Antiquity Street

ANTIQUITY STREET

SONIA RAMI

Farrar Straus Giroux New York

Printed in the United States of America
Published simultaneously in Canada by HarperCollins*CanadaLtd*
First edition, 1992

Designed by Chris Welch

Library of Congress Cataloging-in-Publication Data
Rami, Sonia.
Antiquity Street / Sonia Rami.—1st ed.
p. cm.
I. Title.
PR9375.9.R36A85 1992 823—dc20 91-34564

FOR MINOU, MY MOTHER

Stubborn and proud, I carry my head high;
Haughty by birth, willful,
I would not bow to anything;
I would not even veil my defiant gaze, not I.

But Mother never let me dare deny
How soon my pride, my boastful strength
shamed by your presence and solicitude,
leaves me without one small departing sigh.

Is it your spirit that overpowers me,
Your lofty soul that clears
the earth and cleaves to heaven, flying free.
Memory burns and rankles,
for I know how often I have brought your heart to tears,
The soft and suffering heart that loved me so.

—Heinrich Heine
(author's translation from the German)

AND FOR MY FRIENDS

Richard Sieburth
of Harvard University,
whose poetic sensibility
has illuminated my life

Chava Shafir
of Kibbutz Nachshon,
who gave her son
the Arabic name Ali
as a token of our friendship

ACKNOWLEDGMENTS

I WOULD LIKE to thank my friend the poet and short-story writer Grace Paley, who was the first to read this manuscript and to encourage me to seek its publication. Her political activism and writings—not to mention her immense warmth and kindness, courage and generosity—have always been a source of inspiration for me. My thanks are also due to Helen Wolff, of the Helen and Kurt Wolff book imprint, whose great enthusiasm for the initial draft did a lot for my morale. My friend and literary agent Elaine Markson has my profound gratitude for her inexhaustible stock of patience and loving support. At the beginning, she doubled as editor, taking time off her own hectic schedule to sit with me for hours on end at the Peacock Café, in New York's Greenwich Village, in order to discuss the plot of this book. Later, she weathered with me a crisis in the course of publication, without once uttering an unkind word. My thanks also go to my typist Carol Atkinson, who struggled uncomplainingly with my indecipherable writing and messy manuscript and who always comes through for me. Last but by no means least, I would like to thank my editors Jonathan Galassi and Roslyn Schloss for accepting the manuscript in the first place and for helping me shape it and polish it, once they had committed themselves to it. Any merit this book has is largely due to them; its shortcomings are entirely due to my own inadequacies as a writer.

CONTENTS

Antiquity Street

1

ESCALIER DE SERVICE

I THINK OF Alex always as I first saw him, darting across the corridor that separated our private inner quarters from the reception rooms, his long red silk scarf dancing about his gracefully modeled limbs. So this handsome young man was the *pauvre Grec* Mother had discovered under some tumbledown roof across the bridge, on Antiquity Street, and brought home with her to care for *le pacha*, as she liked to refer to Father. I had tailored Alex to fit his habitat: flaps of loose-hanging, wrinkled skin, underneath which an old man huddled. For were they not all alike, these Greeks whom we spotted in the downtown shopping area, trailing their wretched lives behind them: garlic-scented breath, soiled, sweaty suits. Dregs of the Mediterranean, they had been swept to our shores long ago from the villages and coastal townlets of Greece. White trash, we called them.

I followed Alex down the long corridor to the family living room, where Father sat stiffly upright in his high-backed chair, framed by the many pictures that bore testimony to his extraordinary merit. Father's entire career was laid out on the wall for all to see, beginning with the shot of him as a young man, in gold-embroidered livery, being borne by the royal horse carriage to present his credentials to the King of Sweden, and ending with a shot of him with Gromyko at the United Nations. The bookshelves also exhibited countless mementos: the letter of appointment to an ambassadorship in Washington, D.C., and also to a seat in the Security Council, opening with the words *Nous, Farouk le Roi d'Egypte*; the ivory elephants, a gift of Nehru's; the French Cross of the Legion of Honor, along with various other medals amassed in diplomatic service which, together with the albums of complimentary newspaper clippings, had turned this room into a sanctuary.

Lately, we had spent most of our time in this sanctuary among the tributes to my father, venturing into the salons on the opposite side of the corridor only on rare occasions, when there were visitors. The fancy tea parties and lavish dinners were becoming increasingly a thing of the past, though the simpler fare continued to be served in the sterling silver platters by the gloved *soufragi* with the turbaned head of polished ebony and the cheeks scarred with the markings made by red-hot iron tongs during puberty rites. To be sure, the staff was not nearly as abundant as it had been before the revolution, when, in Mother's words, such people were *bi turab el fulus*, as cheap as dust. In the old days, the Pasha's house had hummed and whirred with the activities of a veritable garrison of servants. These included the stewards reserved for opening the front door and serving at table; the maids reserved for dusting the marble statuette of cupid and porcelain hunting dog, the Sèvres bonbonnières, the cigarette boxes of inlaid ivory, the console tables of black pearwood, the gold-framed rococo mirrors, the flowery Japanese screens, and the innumerable other useless, priceless objects that cluttered salons already encumbered by all the plush, velvet, brocade, silk, and heavy dark furniture; housekeepers, washerwomen, cooks, scullery boys, and chauffeurs. In addition, there were countless children from Mother's estates, who were herded together in the *badrun*, the servants' quarters in the basement, and were assigned specialized tasks, which in the case of the boys consisted of running errands, chasing gray lizards off the walls of the glassed-in southern veranda with a view of the Sporting Club, trampling occasional ants that strayed onto the living room floor—large, indolent brown ants invaded our house every summer—spraying our darkened bedrooms with Flit, against the flies, at siesta time, and fanning Father with a big ostrich-feather fan as he sat in his rattan chair sunning himself and reading the paper; while the girls were responsible for sweeping the Persian carpets twice a day with the long besoms—no matter how often one cleaned in Egypt, one could never quite succeed in getting rid of all the dust released by the sand-laden winds blowing out of the deserts of Africa—changing the water of the dozen or so vases and flower bowls scattered throughout the house, folding the clean laundry, mending clothes, depilating Mother, and massaging her tired feet.

I watched Alex hover anxiously over Father as he

urged himself to the edge of his high-backed rattan chair. Hunched over my father as Alex was, he looked smaller than his actual height, and his spareness, the delicacy of his bones and articulation, lent him a touch of adolescence. His classical nose and firm chin were definitely of Greek cast. He cut a whimsical figure with his perfumed handkerchief lolling at his breast pocket and with his pearl tiepin. How had such a dandy ended up as an orderly in our home, I wondered. To me, it seemed incredible that this man who had burst onto the scene, apparently without a past, should be admitted into our private family wing, from which, ever since I could remember, even close relatives had been barred.

Father heaved himself to a standing position, shaking off Alex's arm irritably as he tried to steady himself on his feeble ankles. I rushed over to grab hold of him; his arm felt as light and brittle as a twig. He had been knocked down by a car and his hip had not healed properly: the doctor had mumbled something about calcification of the bones due to age.

I can't remember when Father's exact age was first revealed to me. It was a subject about which Mother was loath to speak: she was afraid of the evil eye. I remember only the terror that had accompanied me from earliest childhood, the terror that my father would soon die. When I was ten years old I began to notice that his friends were succumbing to heart attacks; Father was already in his sixties then, and I was young enough to regard him as having reached the limit. I prayed God every night before going to bed that Father would live till I was thirteen—which then appeared to me the height of maturity—so that I'd be strong enough to weather the blow. In exchange I promised to be very good—a pact which, needless to say, I found hard to honor. When I reached thirteen I asked God to extend the limit by a few more years. By now, following so many tearful petitions to the Almighty, so much bargaining, so many extensions obtained from the powers beyond, I felt reasonably certain that despite his extreme frailty, the old man would be proof against the vicissitudes of fate to which common mortals had been known to succumb.

To be sure, there had been the accident: as Mother had explained it to me over the phone, when she had urged me to return home, Father simply refused to come to terms with the changing times. He continued to venture forth on his early morning strolls along the bank of the Nile, which our house overlooked, even though the quiet, palm-tree-lined lanes had been overrun since the 1952 revolution by the rabble. *Cochons!* (You swine!)

Mother called out after the unheeding drivers who raced, hooting all the way, down the streets of our once exclusive little island. One such *cochon* had backed into Father, fracturing his hip. And since this new class had none of the delicacy of feeling characteristic of the old, Father had been left lying on the sidewalk. It was the fat black *boab* (doorman) of Park Lane, the building down the street from us, who had found him, after the car made off, and who had waddled, with Father in his arms, all the way to our house, panting and wheezing and calling out in his fluty voice, "The Pasha is dead, the Pasha is dead." At the sight of the *boab*, Mother turned purple with fright and indignation. *Salaud!* (Scoundrel!) she shouted, shaking her fist at the invisible culprit. *Lâche!* (Coward!) And then the most damning epithet of all: *Arriviste!* (Upstart!)

These imposing buildings, bearing the names of a bygone colonial era, had once marked the changeover from the loud vulgarity of the poor neighborhood across the bridge with the shrieks of ragged urchins playing in the gutters, the clangs of the licorice-juice peddlers' metal cups, and the sulky whines of the performing monkeys. Our neighborhood had stood until recently as firmly as a moat holding back this flood of native darkness from its British occupants—only the lighter-skinned members of the Turco-Egyptian aristocracy had succeeded in gaining admission to it.

When my family first moved into the Nile-view building, back in the fifties, next to the palace where Khedive Ismail, the Turkish ruler of Egypt in the late nineteenth century, had hosted Empress Eugénie of France for the festivities marking the inauguration of the Suez Canal —which included the opera *Aida*, especially composed by Verdi for the occasion—most of the houses were still occupied by the likes of Mme Dubonnet and Mrs. Hughes, widows of European entrepreneurs and officials. They complained about the "beastly weather," and though they had chosen to stay on after Egypt's independence, they went on calling Egypt a "bloody hell" until the day Nasser kicked them out, along with all other British and French nationals, after their governments responded to the nationalization of the Suez Canal, in 1956, with a declaration of war. It was to Mrs. Hughes that we owed Father's somber mahogany study with the cuckoo grandfather clock and the uncomfortable Windsor chairs.

The native proprietor of our building had never tried to conceal his blatant partiality for British tenants; he told Mother outright that he would make an "exception" in her case because Father was such a "distinguished"

Egyptian. But now the new moneyed class, those whom the Khedive had condescendingly referred to as his "olive-skinned subjects," had begun leaking into Zamalik at a frightening pace, driving out the impoverished members of the old aristocracy, spoiling the rarefied atmosphere of this island.

It was an atmosphere nowhere so distinct as in this house, set apart by a certain sobriety of taste, a softness of tone, a refinement of manner, and above all by an inordinate amount of culture (with a capital "C"), which we often called to our aid at afternoon teas.

The sweet decadence of this life must have lured Alex to our house, tempting him to give up that precious morsel of freedom he had clung to throughout his impoverished bachelorhood, and to come sleep on the chaise longue in the living room, adjoining Father's bedroom, among the mementos and tributes to his eminence. Alex seemed fascinated by the stacks of starched white sheets with the embroidered pillowcases, impeccably folded by Camille, our Italian housekeeper, by the tidy camphor-smelling closets full of cashmeres, silk scarves, and crocodile purses, by the monogrammed leather kits with the old-fashioned crested stationery. He spent hours going through the buffet drawers with the polished silver in proper rows and the fine linen napkins that were set out daily in elaborate cones before the crystal glasses. Everything matching, everything monogrammed with Father's initial, everything in sets of threes: the guest set and two sets for the house, one for the informal "light" dinners and one for the main meal, which was served punctually at 1:30 p.m.—Father was a fanatic about punctuality. For the former the ordinary china was permissible, but for the latter nothing short of the Sèvres—a family heirloom—would do. And of course the floral centerpieces and lace tablecloths were mandatory. But I forget the fourth set, of glazed pottery, for the servants, which could naturally not be kept in the dining room buffets with ours but had to be placed separately in the pantry.

All these rules—and above all, the feeling of order and well-being emanating from these clean, folded, polished objects—must have given Alex, whose life had in all likelihood been subject to the whims of fate, a measure of security.

I had approached my father with trepidation. On the way home, in the airplane, I had pictured to myself a harrowing encounter: a face ravaged by pain and the approach of death. Or worse still: a late arrival, an empty chair. The sight of that empty chair is what I dreaded above all. My eyes instinctively darted toward it. I was relieved to find Father there, all there, albeit diminished. It was something about his eyes, which were blue as forget-me-nots. The spark was gone from them, and his handsome, pale face was gaunt and worn. As I reached over to place a kiss on his forehead, his hollow cheeks, with the high cheekbones sticking out even more prominently now, came into harsh focus for me; I felt compelled to lower my eyes.

Father's frail arms locked around me with a sort of fusty, trembling eagerness. For a long time he held me thus, tightly, without a word, as though determined not to let me out of his grasp now that I had finally come home. I was surprised at the strength of those wrinkled, wasted arms. He had missed me, missed me terribly, he said.

"*Oui, ma chérie*," Mother concurred, "*il est vrai que parfois tu es assommante, mais tu mets la gaieté à la maison.*" (Yes, it's true you are a nuisance sometimes, but you cheer up the house.) For the Egyptian aristocracy had, ever since Napoleon's invasion of Egypt, considered it chic to intersperse its conversation with some French.

Then she let on that Father had even had an old portrait of mine, which my sister had painted when we were children, brought out of the storage room and hung on the wall opposite his chair.

For a brief moment his blue eyes flickered with some of that old-time mischievous spark. "If only I'd known you wouldn't come back, I'd never have allowed you to go to Harvard!"

"America has made you forget your aging parents," Mother added by way of reproof.

"But," Alex protested, "she calls you long distance every week, Lady Amina!" (He called her that teasingly, mocking her aristocratic pretensions, though his sly humor was quite lost on her.)

Unconsciously I had been observing him, as he brought Father the three stewed prunes he took every evening before going to bed to ensure a good bowel movement the following morning. The way he moved captivated me: he seemed to dance rather than walk in his Italian moccasins. And his purity of line and form, of chin and cheek and brow, imparted to him a kind of effortless grace that made him appear unmistakably a gentleman. The mere contemplation of such perfection seemed to me a privilege; I felt strangely transported—an effect that I later discovered he wrought on people with far greater experience and worldliness than I possessed.

Alex followed me down the corridor, which led to the parlor, where I had deposited my suitcases. (I had tiptoed down that long corridor many times as a child, when distances seem greater than they really are, to eavesdrop from behind the closed door on the snatches of grown-up conversations floating in from the Louis Quinze salons, and then one last time when I turned twenty-one—still a child—to escape the confinement of that womblike enclosure where the world barely reached me as a faint echo, the way it reached harem girls a generation earlier through the wooden lattice windows.)

I sat beside the rosewood side table with the picture of Father in Roosevelt's office. A statuette of Hitler with pins stuck in his bottom was prominently displayed on the American President's desk. I noticed that Alex's eyes ranged carefully over the room's Aubusson set as though he was determined to offer himself only the finest of these chairs, and finally, for reasons known solely to himself, he gave them all up in favor of the gilt-framed bergère decked out in pink brocade into which he settled. While I fumbled with the keys, I was uncomfortably conscious of Alex studying me with a curiosity that bordered on impudence. All at once he asked me, tauntingly, "What is it you love so much about America?" (Like most of Egypt's foreign residents, who were old enough to remember the period of British occupation, Alex was snootily Anglophile; he considered America a boorish, uncultured land.)

I responded somewhat absently, as I was still preoccupied with my search for the keys.

"But what is it you love so much about it?" he reiterated, with a smile that was now distinctly superior.

I hesitated. "The freedom, I suppose," I proffered with a shrug.

"Freedom?" Alex echoed.

"Yeah, yeah, freedom," I said, looking up irritably at him. It was then I caught sight of his eyes, from under the golden darkness of the long curls that fell in profusion over his forehead. He was fixing me with a strange look, a look in which seemed to lurk an intense yearning to grasp the portent of this word.

The next morning I was surprised to find Mother in the dining room; I had been told she had not set foot there since Father's injury, preferring to keep him company while he ate on the sunny, glassed-in veranda overlooking the Sporting Club.

Mother sat with her back to me, stooped over her coffee cup. When she heard me enter, she turned. I realized with a start that it was not Mother but my sister, who it seemed had fallen into the habit of filling Mother's empty chair at mealtimes. She seemed to have aged greatly during the years of my absence, and those added years had heightened her resemblance to Mother. "She's no longer young," I thought to myself with a pang. "She's middle-aged."

I went and sat down opposite her, sat perfectly straight the way my nanny had forced me to sit at table—even insisting that I walk with books under my armpits to correct my posture—as though to prove to myself that at least *I* was not bent over with age. For in observing my sister across the floral centerpiece, I realized that I, too, was past my prime. I was already in my late twenties. Late twenties . . .

My sister's eyes met mine for a moment. I often thought I detected in those eyes flashes of anger bordering on hatred—which, rightly or wrongly, I attributed to her resentment at having had to shoulder a disproportionate share of family responsibility. Had she not nursed Mother during her heart attack while I was off in America pursuing my studies? And after Mother, had there not been a whole series of illnesses which

Father's stubborn vitality had managed to withstand?

I had invited my sister to the States many times. But each time fate had intervened; some new affliction of Father's had pinned her to his bedside. And now, with his hip fracture, it seemed that America was to be once more postponed, perhaps indefinitely.

My sister had always denied that Father was in her way. And Father had given much verbal support to her going, whenever the subject had been raised, taking those opportunities to remind her of all the things he had enjoyed during his ten-year ambassadorial term. Mother, too, had nothing but praise for America; she had felt like *la reine d'Egypte*, the Queen of Egypt, and then to have had to come back and face *ce monstre de Nasser*, who had expropriated her family's lands, and the dreadful dearth of servants . . . No wonder her health had failed her.

I certainly hoped my sister would have the opportunity to come soon, for her sake—the years were going by; she was growing old with Father—and for my own. I could not bear the guilt of being there, of enjoying it all so much. She herself claimed she did not mind being the one to have stayed behind; she always answered me with pathetic hypocrisies about the cultural vitality of

Cairo and all the things to see and do there. And Mother, who was brought up on the notion that a woman should sacrifice herself for her husband, saw no reason why my sister, *une vraie perle*—a real pearl—should not do the same for her father. Mother looked upon a trip to America as something for which there was all the time in the world, and upon my sister's presence with Father as something that could not be postponed. Mother had herself been ailing for years, but Father's health, in ministering to which she had devoted so much of her life, had left her no time to take care of herself. And now it was too late.

I knew Mother to be altruistic to a fault, and I understood all too well how torn she must be between her sense of duty to her husband and her love and pity for her daughter, who was, as she put it, growing into a *vieille fille*, an old maid, by his bedside. But I could not help feeling there was a kind of placid perversity in her statement that my sister would go "in good time."

"Mother, she won't have any time, she doesn't have much time left," I had once put it to her bluntly.

"Just think how the girl would feel if something were to happen to your father while she was away," she replied.

"Ho, ho, fat chance!" I snickered.

"How can you say such an awful thing!" Mother cried out.

"The only thing that's awful is the age the 'girl' is reaching," I replied icily and walked out of the room.

After the meal, I joined my parents on the glassed-in southern veranda, where I found Alex serving Father a breakfast tray laden with the prescribed delicacies to which his station in life had accustomed him. Father had been propped up against the crimson cushion of his elegant, stiff-backed rattan chair. His prominent high cheekbones now made his vulpine nose appear longer and more pointed. In these curious features there was a suggestion of a lengthy genetic transmission, of an organism highly evolved, of class. And this, combined with the dauntless expression of his small blue eyes, lent his intensely aged face the mummified look of a regal bird of prey in a cage.

I gave Mother a peck on the cheek and nestled close to her on the love seat, draping my arm affectionately around her shoulder. She seemed to be gravely studying the flame tree that brushed against the windowpane. After a few minutes, during which she sat silently while

I chatted idly with Father and Alex, she exclaimed in Arabic, as though pursuing an inner monologue of her own, "*Dunya!*" (What a world!) When I asked her what the matter was, she told me that the tree reminded her of the old days when Father had a cabinet post and a gardener would be sent periodically to our house by the municipality to inquire if we would like it pruned so it would not obstruct our view of the club. "You see, my daughter," she added, with a deep sigh, "everyone has his moment."

Alex reverted to the subject of America. He wanted to know what I had seen of it.

"Not nearly as much as I'd have liked to, only California. It's very pretty, but it just hasn't got the cultural vitality of New England."

After a moment's reflection, I told him he should come visit me sometime in Boston.

"Do you really mean that?" he exclaimed, his voice vibrating with dread and desire.

"Of course! I always speak my mind. Haven't my parents told you how impossibly blunt I am?" I said, laughing. "And who knows . . . you might end up liking it so much you'll decide to stay on. It's been known to happen!"

"Stay on?" he whispered, as though the sheer audacity of this thought had cut his breath short.

Was it just my imagination, or did I spot a look of reproach in Father's cold blue stare?

At any rate, I thought it prudent to drop the subject. For the next few moments I watched Alex in silence. He was basking in the sun, swinging back and forth on the rocking chair, stealing an occasional glance at his beautifully arched foot as he played with his leather sandals. He had about him the slightly blasé air of one who had plumbed satiation and had exhausted pleasures.

How could this indolent, catlike man weather the harsh discipline of our home: up at five every day to prepare breakfast for Father—often after a sleepless night spent listening to him recounting and embellishing some episode of his career—having to contend with his endless demands, with his fastidiousness, and his tantrums when his orders were not carried out just so? Was it not trying for Alex to be confined to the company of this wraithlike being, who alternated between fits of indomitable anger and displays of pride in feats that had taken place fifty years before? Perhaps Alex had come because he felt safe in our house. The Egypt in which he had spent most of his adult life, Nasser's Egypt, had been full of difficulties, even dangers, for the foreigner, and as the Greeks began to emigrate, Alex must have been deprived of the compensations which his European neighborhood's clannish call to solidarity had provided him with. Here with us he felt secure in the knowledge that no matter how indifferently the Pasha might treat him, he would come to his aid if Alex was ever confronted with difficulties or dangers.

Even before his accident, I had not known Father to so much as get out of his chair to fetch himself a glass of water. Prior to Alex's coming, it had been Mother who had had to cater to his insatiable demand for her attention and her energy. He was a typical Egyptian husband: he had all the exigencies of one who had never had to lift a finger for himself in his life. The morning after the wedding, he lost no time in instructing his bride in her new duties; she had to wrench herself out of her sleep to prepare his elaborate breakfast, which he liked to have served to him in bed at six-thirty on the dot by her in person, since he could not suffer the presence of a servant in his room at that hour.

From then on the treadmill continued. While Father was calmly savoring his croissant in bed she would have to rush to the bathroom to pick up the towels which we children, who were the first to bathe in order to be ready for the school bus, had thrown on the floor, and to replace them with clean towels. For if there was one thing Father abhorred, it was the sight of limp, damp towels.

Indeed, he could not tolerate the slightest disorder. He liked to see the towels before him starched, well pressed—their spotless white linen smelling of the flatiron—hanging in neat little rows by the sink and bathtub. His bathroom had to be immaculate: if there was the smallest blotch on the glass shelf where his shaving brush stood, caused by one of us inadvertently splashing water onto it, he would let out a howl upon entering the bathroom which, while it had long ceased to frighten us children, would send the servants scrambling for shelter behind the kitchen doors. Mother's perpetual chain of duties ended only when she turned in, after she had carefully tucked the hot water bottle under Father's bedspread in the winter, or filled the bottle with ice chunks if it was summer. Even then she could not quite allow herself to fall asleep; she would often creep out of bed anxiously after he had begun to snore, to make sure she had not forgotten to put a bottle of Perrier in the refrigerator, in case he woke up thirsty during the night, and to take out his morning compote, which he did not like to eat cold.

In his love for order, truth, and punctuality, Father

was most untypical of Egypt, and my mystified mother had long ago concluded that this quirk in his nature was a vestige of his Macedonian ancestry. Nothing vexed Mother so much as father's tyrannical call for perfection: if the leg of lamb was one shade darker than the desired pink, or his steak was the slightest bit overdone, he would have no compunction about creating a scandal in any plush restaurant in Paris or on the Riviera by calling for the maître d'hôtel and asking in a loud voice, within ear range of the fancy clientele, "*Dites, monsieur! C'est une mauvaise plaisanterie, ça, ou quoi? Veuillez ôter tout de suite cette semelle de chaussure de devant moi!*" (I say, Maître, is this a bad joke, or what? Kindly remove this shoe sole immediately from in front of me!)

In time, Mother's health had caved in. The change had been so slow as to be almost imperceptible, but when it became apparent that she was dragging her once lithe body down our long corridor—along with the heavy necklace of precious stones, Father's betrothal gift, which she had worn throughout her cheerless married life—it was my sister who rallied to the call.

Her strong sense of duty and family obligation had made her instinctively hostile to my concept of free will and self-development. I had rejected the Oriental notion that children were brought into this world to sacrifice themselves for their parents, and had run off to the States to free myself from the Egyptian tangle of conventions and prejudices.

Alex, clearly, was stunned by the boldness of my life. He, who so desperately yearned for the respectability that came with an abundance of objects clean, folded, polished, and stacked, was awed by my positive distaste for the good stuff: the excess of cashmere, crocodile, and handmade silks in our closets, the fine porcelains, the legs of lambs with smoky gravies, and the shrimp flown in from the Red Sea coast. He had never met someone with both the money and the servants to carry out such extreme expressions of style who had rebelled against the canon which decreed that the glasses had to be placed above the knife—always to the right of the soup spoon—and that the salad dish must go on the left, *above* the fork.

Secretly, I was proud, of course, of the distinction my father had attained. It had been drummed into me from earliest infancy that Father's mail bore the insignia *H.E.* for His Excellency, that he was descended from an Ottoman general who, when he defeated the British troops at the port of Rosetta, in 1805, had been rewarded with the governorship of Alexandria. That Father's father, a pasha, had, on account of his distinguished reputation as the Dean of Cairo University's faculty of medicine, been chosen by the Khedive to be his private physician (a great honor, since before this only Europeans were selected for the post). That Father's uncle, who brought him up because my grandfather died when Father was only seven years old, had been Prime Minister of Egypt and had married the daughter of the Ottoman Sultan Abd el Hamid's chief of staff, a young girl imported from Turkey for the wedding.

When I dwelt on all the notable particularities of this magnificent family chronicle, I had no doubt at all that I, the daughter and granddaughter of pashas, was charged with advancing the brilliance of the family through my marriage.

In her effort to press me into the role of glorified servitude, Mother never tired of offering me the example of the Prophet Muhammad's daughter. She was so considerate, Mother said, that every evening she would ready a basin of warm water to wash her husband's feet when he returned home, along with his cane, in case he wanted to beat her—so he would not have to look for it when he was tired from work. Alas! I had failed in the role of the accomplished daughter, disappointing Mother, who had projected onto me all the aborted dreams of her own frustrated youth. My Harvard education and my career ambitions were but poor substitutes for a husband. What Mother would have preferred would have been a wedding that ensured me a role of arrogant ease and leisure: having my hands kissed by the servants, being attended to by a posse of tailors, dressmakers, and manicurists, ordering my underlings about in the morning, and impressing my peers at the yacht club in the evening, by a brilliant display of the latest fashions acquired on my most recent trip to Europe. But I had simply refused to be yet another Egyptian woman with the lifeless perennial bloom of a doll that has been penciled, dyed, and painted for her husband—not a single thought or experience discernible beneath those coats of paint. And I had thrown away my chance to be a "kept" woman—and a rich one—by wrecking my marriage with a *monsieur très distingué*. Out of filial affection, I had tried very hard to see him through Father's eyes, but I had failed to discern in him more than a lusterless, unimaginative public servant of unimpeachable probity and good breeding. In the end I had felt compelled to reject this marriage of accommodation: I could not go on presenting to the world a united front which I alone knew was not really cemented but merely soldered together by good manners and convention.

How, I wondered in retrospect, had I ever been induced to make my vows of love to a man who wanted me for his wife only because, as the daughter of a pasha, I was a social adornment? In the restorative solitude after my divorce, I had rediscovered the pleasure of living at my body's bidding, eating only when I was hungry, going to sleep only when I was tired, possessed at last of the right to my own bed, where I could love without lies or simply make love alone until my body was satisfied with dreaming its own voluptuous dreams and I awoke refreshed.

Thereafter I had disgraced my family by engaging in a series of scandalous affairs. And then there had been that brief, delightful interlude in Berlin that I had lived out not as a woman but as the man—which perhaps I ought to have been. Ever since I had turned my back on all I knew to cast my lot with a single girlfriend, Mother had come to look on me as one who had vanished not just out of our home and our family but out of life itself.

Off I had gone afterward to America, where I had discovered it was possible to survive without servants. And now nothing in the world could induce me to give up the beauty of the freedom of my life there. To be sure, it was not a model of felicity. But who was to say I would have been happier on the island of Zamalik in a luxury penthouse, with a view of the Nile, full of those bucolic tapestries and gilt-framed brocaded chairs that were the ordained dowry of every young girl *de bonne famille*?

Alex surely had to agree with Lady Amina when she stated that her daughter was *scandaleuse*. Imagine getting up at noon and running about the house barefoot, in stained shirts and tattered jeans! The one or two times she had succeeded in getting her daughter into a proper dress, for a dinner party, then, instead of sitting cross-legged in the salon, one hand resting gracefully in the palm of the other, a smile glued to my lips and a beatific expression glazing my eyes—the way girls of good families were supposed to do—I had shamed my parents by yawning in the faces of important people and by making improper remarks at table, punctuating them with squeals of laughter.

I suspect Alex did not quite know what to make of this "impossible creature." Yet in a way, I think, he admired me: perhaps I kept alive in him, who had never dared imagine an alternate life for himself, the dream that it was possible to make a choice. At any rate, he was glad I refused to play the role of the charming hostess—the well-mannered daughter of a pasha—by rejecting the pretensions of those formal dinners, with their affected table etiquette, their staged candlelit settings and conversations across floral centerpieces, from which he was excluded on account of his class.

Once I had begged Mother to allow Alex to join us for high tea. But when he entered the salon, not one of the young gentlemen in the white flannel trousers and black Oxfords—relics of their student days in England—deigned to let their hands so much as come within touching distance of his as they greeted him, nor did a single smile hail from the corner bridge tables where young women had settled down in a flurry of pastel cottons, pale silks, and bright georgettes. Tongue-tied and self-conscious, Alex sat among these friends of mine who were confident, handsome, and brashly opinionated as they joked across the tables. So that later when the servants came in to clear the Delft porcelain tea set and the serving dishes of petits fours and fondants, I was at pains to disguise my embarrassment over the wounds I knew had been inflicted on his self-esteem. How vulnerable he seemed once he had sloughed off that tough, non-caring look he wore in front of others!

It was his first experience of social snobbery in our house—a snobbery complicated by the fact that he stood, by virtue of his white skin, in a position far superior to that of the native members of the staff, even if my parents had felt compelled to place him at the very bottom rung of their own self-contained society. They did not believe that people could ever transcend their class; they held that the stamp of one's origins was indelible.

I myself had always disapproved of my family's preoccupation with class; I felt it made life unnecessarily difficult. Even Mother must have thought so at times, because she seemed hard put to know what expression to wear when addressing Alex, which must have accounted for her look of extreme exasperation at having to talk to him at all. Speaking of him to others, Mother usually referred to *notre larbin grec* (our Greek flunky), but she addressed him as *garçon* (boy), and in rare moments of gratitude, when Alex had sat up all night seeing Father through another of his bouts of insomnia or had administered an enema or performed some other unsavory task, Mother would shed the cold, dissatisfied look she habitually adopted in the presence of servants and would tell him, "*Vous êtes comme mon fils*"—You are like my son—and permit him to come sit with us at dinner.

About Alex's life we knew very little beyond his obvious poverty. I did try to prod him gently once or twice, but he remained cryptic and courteous behind that amiable expression that you were not supposed to see past: I could not learn anything from him by indirection and I did not dare ask him outright. He had nothing but the name of a city—Alexandria—for background, and a conviction that he belonged to an ancient and glorious race. It had been inculcated in him from childhood that there was grandeur in his past, and when he reached high-school age he received confirmation thereof from an authoritative old volume that he tremblingly and exultantly consulted in the library.

I tried to imagine what it meant for him to have a Greek heritage, that heritage of which he was so fiercely proud without knowing anything about it—his entire cosmopolitan experience consisted of one trip to Cyprus—and to have grown up in a city like Alexandria at a time when it was so paradoxically Levantine in its Westernness.

No one could have conformed more to the image evoked by "Levantine." Alex had a little cleverness, a little reading, a little Arabic and French, and an immense amount of male vanity. He was far from being an incarnation of the Greek ideal. He was a typical product of an old, corrupt, exhausted civilization, with no moral standards save through imitation and no opinions save through tradition and superstition.

Mother once opined that she suspected Alex was not *très comme il faut*: not very proper. (I remember how she went on paring her apple as she said that, with an expression that managed to be at one and the same time speculative and indifferent.) That was the closest she would come to permitting herself a compromising remark. People's private lives were never talked about in my family. Discretion, tact, privacy—these were sacrosanct values. Privacy above all. To talk about things of a more intimate nature would have been unthinkable, even to one's children. Especially to one's children.

The closest I had come to uncovering the mysteries of sex as a small child was seeing my father's jockstrap, distended with the shape of his huge balls, in the bathroom where he showered in the morning after his game of golf at the Sporting Club. I don't believe I had ever seen Father in so much as pajamas: he always emerged from his bedroom fully dressed—tie and all. The fact that lower-middle-class Egyptians lazed about their apartments in their pajamas till all hours of the day represented for him a contemptible *manque de tenue*, a lack of restraint. *Tenue* was everything in our house, because it denoted breeding; the highest compliment my parents could bestow on someone was to say of him that he was *très comme il faut*.

Alex was certainly not *comme il faut*. He lounged about the living room in his sumptuous silk dressing gown and extravagant Japanese slippers, in a faint but unmistakable cloud of citrus-scented eau de cologne for men, Egoïste by Chanel, bantering with Father, playing poker with Mother, all the while gracefully smoking Cleopatras, almost as a woman might smoke them, yet with such an air of lethal male self-assurance that only the most foolhardy would have leaped to any conclusions. Previously, he would never have been hired. But in these hard times, when the lack of servants was the primary concern of every self-respecting Egyptian housewife, when Nasser had stuffed the heads of the common folk with all kinds of ideas, and the slogan *Irfa ra'sak ya akhi*—raise up your head, brother—was painted on every wall, when the sons of cooks could be seen sitting next to the sons of former pashas in the now tuition-free universities, no one wanted to be a servant anymore. So my parents had had to bend their standards a little and hire Alex, and even allow him to sit with us in the living room, though Mother was the first one to admit, "*Auparavant cet homme n'aurait été admis chez nous que par les escaliers de service!*" (Only a few years ago, this man would have been admitted to our presence only by way of the service stairs!")

2

LORD OF THE MANOR

IT WAS NOT ONLY Alex whom we had to make room for in our home but, in rapid succession, Alex's female cat, Agrapimou (my little man)—whom he took everywhere with him—his flea-ridden mutt, his parrot, who spoke only Greek, his lame pigeon and one-eyed owl, and even a family of mice that he had adopted and kept in a cage well out of the cat's reach. (My mother not only tolerated their presence but turned a blind eye when he fed them morsels of our expensive imported French cheese—all this despite the fact that none of us had been allowed pets as children because she feared for her Persian carpets.)

I had had the occasion to witness many times how Alex worked his magic on animals, when we went out together in the afternoon while Father napped. He would walk down the street whistling and chirping, trailed by an ever-growing number of homeless four-legged creatures—and, much to my embarrassment, by an ever-growing number of fellow humans who pointed and laughed at us. While Alex did not hold his own kind in high esteem, he was inordinately fond of animals. I have never seen him so irate as the day he caught sight of some street louts amusing themselves by aiming pebbles with slings at birds on a tree. Once when he found a baby sparrow that had been injured in this fashion, he brought it home and, after nursing it to health, climbed up the tree to place it back in the nest out of which it had fallen. Another time he crawled on his stomach underneath a parked car and spent nearly ten minutes coaxing some emaciated kitten, which had taken refuge there, to come out. In the end, the kitten found Alex's chirping irresistible—she remains part of our household to this day. He also had a special relationship with dogs: they obeyed him instantly, as if hypnotized by the extraordinary charm of his face and voice.

The arrival of Alex late at night followed by a whole procession of pariah dogs always caused consternation in our quarters because the gaunt black *boab*, a devout Muslim, who sat by the main door all day on an old tire, smoking his nargileh and squinting fiercely with his one eye at intruders, believed dogs' wet muzzles were *nagis* (impure) and that he must run and perform his ablutions the moment he came into contact with one. Quite naturally, he resented having to rouse himself from his state of bemused inertia.

Alex's mission to provide a shelter for Cairo's thousands of pariah dogs—victims of an ingrained Muslim prejudice against them that made them a ready target for stones—was cut short one day when Mother returned home from shopping to find a creature that looked human in its helpless misery, but which she hesitated to name, installed in her salon, on her delicate bergère upholstered in pink silk brocade. The dog, which feebly raised its head and stared at her vacantly, was also pink because it had lost all its hair and its raw skin was exposed. Had Mother not then firmly laid down the rule that Alex's conversations with the dogs must come to an end at our front door and that the visitations of the cats—each and every one of which was individually known to him by a Greek name—must be confined to our service stairs, where he would be permitted to serve them bread soaked in milk twice a day, our home would have come to resemble the Humane Society.

Sentimental, tough, comic, irritating, infinitely endearing—that was Alex. To the pets had been added, at first surreptitiously and then ever more brazenly, a whole succession of flowering cacti, potted palms, and other tropical shrubs that changed our sober abode into a chaotic garden of Eden.

Against the chalky white walls of the northern veranda, overlooking the Nile, there exploded a host of vermilion, fuchsia, golden, and purple blossoms, not carefully contained in vases but spilling over exuberantly, cascading, bursting out of the very seams of the clay pots, which were ensconced in the corners of the room and lined the railing. They flowered in wanton abandon, having nothing in common with the well-cut, disciplined bouquets that Mother, who had been trained in the minor decorative arts: flower arrangements, table setting, still-life paintings—all the things deemed useful for an upper-class girl of her generation to know—had placed in the Limoges bowls of the adjacent salon.

By now relatives and friends who hadn't visited us in years had begun to flock to our place in order to take a look at the exotic hothouse flower in our employ. I couldn't help thinking at times that Alex ought to resent being served up for the entertainment of these fine people, who were all style and no content, yet somehow he didn't. Perhaps he felt that if it weren't for this kind of attention, his flimsy presence would go unnoticed by his social betters. Even Father—that silent, dignified man who had learned during his long diplomatic career to renounce the friendship of ordinary human beings in favor of their deference—seemed to relish Alex's petty volubility and vulgar jokes. He, who in the past had been pleased enough with the knowledge that he was more respected and feared by his underlings than liked, now outdid himself to win over Alex.

I, too, reveled in his noisy exuberance. I had been born into my parents' middle age. My family had wanted only peace and quiet; after my brother and sister were born they had neither expected nor desired a third child. And when the cod liver oil followed by the hot showers, which Mother had been taking on a friend's advice, failed to rid her of me, she proceeded to rob me, almost from birth, of that childhood which had been promised me by nature, through her disapproval of everything and everyone I brought into the house that threatened to disturb the serene sanctuary she had created for Father. *Veux-tu rester tranquille!* (Will you be still!) was Mother's most frequent exhortation throughout my childhood years.

My sister objected to the way we all preened and fluttered about Alex—*un homme quelconque*, a common man. And since she could not fathom his triviality, she did not deign to address a word to him. But I was enchanted by him, coarse and unlettered though he was. Lacking a real education, he tended to pick up from Egyptian tabloids ideas that had been circulating in America for at least a decade and to proclaim them as though they were brand-new. Had he been ugly, I might not have been able to listen to him for long, but his good looks redeemed even his French accent—he spoke French in that trailing singsong manner characteristic of the Levant—lending color to his banal conversation and weight to his biased opinions. He took politics no more seriously than he did the Zamalik-Ahli football games, and unlike my Harvard friend Richard, who admired the breadth of my interests and was delighted when I showed off my literary wares to impress him, Alex was supremely indifferent to anything cultural. With him I discussed the merits not of Rimbaud or Nerval but of Princess Di's latest hairdo or Marilyn Monroe's breasts—*les plus beaux nénés du cinéma* (the best tits in the movie business)—according to Alex—*de quoi remplir les mains d'un honnête homme* (enough to fill an honest man's hands).

Besides old movies, his only interest was in knick-knacks, which he liked to collect. We often went for walks at siesta time: our conversations were confined to the dilapidated sidewalks and sinuous alleys of Cairo, the only places that afforded us some privacy. We were not likely to run into anyone we knew: during those sleepy afternoon hours, the streets were owned by beggars and flies. Alex would stop before some shop window with a bewildering assortment of cheap china, lumpish ivory work, wooden cigarette boxes with stodgy decorations, and gaudy porcelain chandeliers. After a long, contemplative halt, he would pick out some objects I found tawdry. I had no compunctions about telling him straight off I thought them hideous, as I knew that nothing I said would offend him. Though his taste was bad beyond measure, his pretension to cultivated judgment was equally great. On those rare occasions when we happened to come on a fragment of antique pottery or an Arab mosaic piece and I extolled its delicacy, he would hoot with derision and declare that he wouldn't want it even if it were offered to him free of charge.

Once, when I had been lucky enough to find a piece of Greco-Roman marble for sale, he told me I should give it to him: he would put it to good use in the public toilets of Egypt, where there was often a shortage of paper. He alleged that poor people routinely carried flat stones in their pockets to use after defecation. On a recent trip by Pullman to Suhag, in southern Egypt, he had been puzzled by the sight of scores of men hurling themselves out of their third-class compartments, stones in hand, whenever the train pulled into a stop. Later he learned that the lucky passenger who had boarded first had barricaded himself inside the toilet for the duration of the trip, leaving the others no choice but to squat on the tracks under their galabias.

In this way, Alex gave rein to his impulse to pull down what was above him. But secretly he was fascinated by my ability to discriminate between the fine and the gross, and often, after we had left a shop, he would return obliquely to the subject of his purchase and try to find out from me, by indirection, wherein lay the superiority, which much to his annoyance he couldn't see, of one object over another. As for myself, even though the particular souvenir he had chosen might excite my disgust, I was actually delighted to discover that some people survived without living off works of art: for too long I had been able to respond only to brilliant, erudite men.

At that time, I still found it difficult to sort out the

bewildering emotions Alex produced in me. At bottom I liked him, strangely, absurdly, but only well enough to tease and torment him—his ego took it all so well. How fond Alex was of me then I could not venture to guess. He teased me back. Our relationship progressed along a bumpy course marked by taunts and defiance.

Perhaps Alex's hold on me also had something to do with his vitality, that cocksureness that comes naturally in Egypt to one born the right gender. Our house needed a man. Father was no longer there; the shell of him was there. The same man, it is true, the same dignified, proud man, seemed to preside over our daily life. But in a horrifying way, everything had changed. The living room was still kept as a sanctuary for him, Mother saw to it that his bed was as carefully made as ever and that his food was prepared with the same fastidious care, but it was as though he had grown indifferent to the crisp comfort of his Swiss linen sheets, and he could no longer make distinctions between the stuffed pigeon, the tips of whose delicate limbs were encircled by silvery paper frills, and the sea bass, whose eyes were shrouded with black olive skins and whose mayonnaise-covered back was studded with caviar and baby shrimps. Even the crepes suzette, daubed with his favorite cognac and served in a wreath of blue flames, failed to revive his spirits. To be sure, something ate with us, and occasionally roused itself to answer our questions, but no, he wasn't there. He himself recognized this. He had once said to me, "*Je suis un mort vivant*": I am a living dead man.

It was from this grim, decaying presence, waiting in its high-backed chair, that Alex's childlike, almost violent exuberance was such a refuge. One could not but be struck by the fund of life that was in him, the energy of feeling—his joie de vivre. These qualities far outweighed for me his limited acquaintance with literature and even his execrable taste.

At home, Alex and I settled into the roles we had written for ourselves, he lord of the manor, bullying and coaxing the domestic staff as he passed on Father's orders to them, and I lady of the manor, sailing out every morning into the shopping area of 26th of July Street (known before the revolution as King Fuad Street), where, without deigning to get out of the car, I would order the chauffeur to bid the salesmen bring their wares to me, which, after tasting, smelling, fingering, disarranging, I would often reject. Not haughtily but with that gracious, self-assured manner of the high-born, who feel that it is their right to impose upon the forbearance of the common people, whose troubles are adequately compensated by a charming, convivial flow of small talk (the very same stock of bright, meaningless, set phrases about the weather, health, and the like that later in the day I would draw on in our salons to greet my parents' friends, with whom I talked only the most complete nonsense).

Thus, thanks to Alex, I came to be reconciled to my life in Egypt—and even enjoyed it. Only a short while before, when I returned home, I had thought I would be unable to endure for long the prospects that presented themselves to me on the drive in from the airport to Zamalik. Cairo had seemed poorer than I remembered, dirtier, drabber, more crowded. Masses of people milled about the two majestic lions, dating back to British colonial times, that guarded the entrance to the Kasr el Nil Bridge. There was no forward movement in them, even the air felt stale here—all but exhausted. And the waters of the Nile appeared a turbid gray, beneath the haze of pollution.

I had stared at the street on the other side of the bridge; only if truly pushed was I prepared to recognize it as my own! During the years I had been away from Egypt, the handsome old mansions on the island seemed to have crumbled; inside their gates, what were once beautiful gardens now spread unkempt, in shaggy desolation. Even the better-kept, modern buildings had been marred by the unskillful introduction of air-conditioning units, which had opened cracks in their whitewashed walls. The handsome corniche along the Nile had all but vanished under the onslaught of Mercedeses—insolently double-parked right on top of our curb. And the ardent smell of roses in the Andalusian Park by the riverbank, where I used to play as a child, was all but buried behind that of open sewers.

What two decades of Nasser's "socialist revolution" had not succeeded in accomplishing, Sadat had brought about in only a few years of his economic "open-door policy." The impoverished old aristocracy had been run out of the Zamalik by hordes of shady speculators and unscrupulous middlemen—the *nouveaux riches* of Egypt. This once exclusive island now resembled any downtown area, with the same littered sidewalks and noisy, congested pavements. Even my own house was alien to me: its run-down, old-fashioned furnishings were a shock; they seemed familiar, but not nearly as grand as they were in the place I had reserved for them in my memory.

My first night, I did not sleep: I have a vague recollection of swatting at mosquitoes and of ramming my pillow against my ears to stifle the squawks of the lizards in heat on the veranda walls and the all-night howls of street cats in our service stairs. Finally, in the morning, I slipped from tossing dreams of America into a waking nightmare—my repugnance at everything Egypt had to offer: the punishing heat, the stench of the river that invaded my bedroom, the shrill cries outside my window of the ambulant peddlers of secondhand wares in search of useless old sticks of furniture, buried amid the dust and cobwebs of the attics of this rich neighborhood, that they could resell to the poor people across the river (the din they made was enough to wake up the whole city). I was convinced that I did not have the heart to live one more day in my rubbish-strewn homeland.

But little by little, under the spell of Alex's friendship, I grew accustomed to the inexorable climate, to the rancid street odors, to the hasty judgments and ingrained prejudices of friends and family, to their vicious gossip, to the tomorrow *in sha' Allah*, until at last the enchantment of my new life with him completely erased the bitterness of my first impression. For though our interests and tastes were very different, in the magical ease of our nascent friendship Alex and I felt something was promised us.

On the weekends, Alex's days off, he began sometimes to take me down to Alexandria, his birthplace, where he introduced me to the delights of the sun, the warm sand, and the cool touch of sea spray on one's cheeks. Upon arriving in the city, we would ride the rusty little trolleys with the squeaking wheels, past stops that echoed the legends of bygone days: Camp de César, San Stefano, Lawrence, Glymonopoulos, Rushdi Pasha (named after my great-uncle, who was Prime Minister during World War I), Chatby, my school stop. The name irresistibly brought back the memory of a certain conductor who made a great impression on small girls by exposing his virile member. Emboldened by the presence of our chums, and often on a dare, we would gigglingly enter his little steering cab, only to flee from there moments later squealing with laughter and terror, without ever working up enough courage to take a close-up look at the monster.

When we arrived at the Stanley Bay front we would get out and walk ankle-deep in the foaming sea until we reached the old palace on Muntazah Beach where King Farouk had signed my father's letter of appointment to Washington, in 1943—I can still see the traces of Alex's shapely feet on the deserted shore. Then we would sit under a big awning fringed with red tassels, on Cleopatra Beach, and we would breakfast on a honeyed wafer, which we bought from vendors calling out "*Fresca, fresca*" (a word whose poetry recalled the days when most of Alexandria's bakers were Italians). We would await the arrival of the mothers with their children followed by a phalanx of turbaned menservants carrying colorful parasols and fly whisks, as well as heavy picnic boxes and crates filled with chunks of ice, lemonades, and Cokes. Some of the women wore bikinis, while others swam fully dressed, veils and all, having succeeded in throwing off the yoke of Western civilization.

Our dinner usually consisted of a *semit*, a soft sesame pretzel, dipped in *dukkah*, a concoction of Oriental spices, which we ate seated under an oleander in Nouzha, the rose garden where E. M. Forster allegedly had his love affair with an Egyptian train conductor. But sometimes Alex and I would drive up to Zephyrion, a Greek taverna, in Abukir, where Napoleon's fleet had landed when he attempted to conquer Egypt, for a special meal of sea urchins. If Alex had a weakness it was for sea urchins, and at Zephyrion this luxury was cheap and abundant.

Once I proposed that we dine instead in my family's resort home in Sidi Kreir, which lay on the outskirts of Alexandria, in a coastal strip of the Western Desert dotted with the Muslim shrines and Coptic monasteries that had supplanted earlier ascetic communities of pagans, Jews, and Christians. Sidi Kreir had been named after a Muslim holy man, who settled there during the wave of Bedouin migration from the Libyan deserts in the last century. Next to his shrine, overlooking Lake Mareotis, a salt lake, were the winter homes of some of Egypt's European residents, who came for the bird-hunting season, while ours, an Arab house, lay to the north, wedged in between the salt lake and the sea. It consisted of a single, dome-roofed living area, overlooking the marble fountain of an inner courtyard, flanked on both sides by barrel-vaulted loggias with built-in *mastabas* (stone benches) for sleeping.

Many years before, when the world-renowned architect Hassan Fathy was still an obscure young man with somewhat eccentric tastes for an Egyptian, he had spotted, in the course of a drive along a desolate shoreline, a small spring that seemed to have burst miraculously out of the desert. It was tucked away behind a sand dune, within a stone's throw of a lonely beach. Instantly, the young man's imagination began to endow this barren strip of land with fig and palm trees, which would set down roots where the pure water ran and would circle around a simple, white, round stone house capped with a dome patterned after the domes of the Sultan Hassan and Rifa'i mosques, which his own seventeenth-century house in Old Cairo overlooked. And he had indeed succeeded, by virtue of his indefatigable zeal, in coaxing lush vegetation out of the desert, by channeling the spring along the seed beds, guiding it finally into the marble cistern that formed the base of the water fountain in the center of the courtyard.

It was that house he had offered my family as a present. The courtyard with its exuberant tropical vegetation, which lent us shade as we sat on the white stone benches, and its graceful fountain, which soothed our spirits, was really the mainstay of the building. Not only did it provide passage from one part of the house to the other, but my family's life unfolded there. We read, played canasta and backgammon, ate; and sometimes, when it was very hot, my sister and I even slept there until an invisible sheet of dew covered us and awoke us at dawn, sending us inside, shivering, to seek shelter.

Even now, when this sprightly octogenarian came for visits, he remained frightfully jealous of us for the little green things that owed their life to his loving care and devotion.

For me, the true splendor of the stone house lay in its simple and lucent perfection of form. The austerity of its bare white walls was countered by magnificent slotted views, through the wrought-iron windows, of the emerald wash of the tides on the shore. Alex could hardly contain his joy when I showed it to him; he ran ecstatically from window to window snatching a view of the sea gulls skirting the foaming sea, taking in the wild strength of the wind-tossed desert, which itself resembled a tumultuous ocean, its waves of dunes rolling into the seething waters.

Afterward, we had gone and sat out on the sand, beside a campfire, under the gigantic red evening whose reflections bled away in the sea. All around us was darkness, a darkness fitfully lit by the small kerosene stoves far away, on which fish, their entrails packed with garlic and cumin, were being cooked. It seemed peaceful enough from where we sat; only if one listened intently could one detect the hum of voices hailing from the distant desert encampments, where Bedouins, whose ancestral common grazing lands had been seized by the army and turned into a summer resort for soldiers, had regrouped, and the faint sound of laughter. How merrily Egypt laughed away its problems, past and present!

Occasionally the flare of our crackling logs illuminated momentarily, with a sudden burst of brilliance, the passing figures of Bedouin boys toting slings, dead birds strung along their belts. Their carriage, the gestures of their small, grimy hands were unbelievably refined, courtly; their faces with the finely chiseled features suggested the frozen silhouettes in the friezes of the pharaonic burial chambers.

Alex grew loquacious after a few beers: his conversation, as we sat and rolled out a dough of dates and flour, Bedouin style, which we cooked over the open fire, was full of the debris of the lives of people he had known who had since emigrated. He would reminisce, tears streaming down his face, about his old school friend Pano, who had left for Australia after Nasser nationalized his father's cigarette factories, abolished all remaining foreign business privileges—residuals of colonial times—and passed a law compelling the children of foreign residents to learn Arabic at school (prior to Nasser, the Greek schools, like other foreign schools, were exempted from the teaching of Arabic, which foreigners, who used it only for exchanges with their servants, did not deem worthy of serious attention).

Pano's father had owned one of the winter homes in this area, a splendid old mansion, according to Alex, who used to spend his vacations there as a boy. Alex had first met Pano on the basketball court of the Greek school in Alexandria they both attended, and he had been instantly taken by this fair young man with the graceful physique and a complexion honeyed by sea bathing. Though the other boys often made fun of Pano's finicky walk and precarious refinement, Alex admired everything about him: he compared the generous warmth and extravagance of Pano's winter residence, and its elegance, to the dull comforts of his house with its cumbersome, featureless furniture, Pano's dignified bearing and easy self-assured manner to his own diffident, ungainly walk and petulant expression, and the way Pano spoke, in a low, modulated tone of voice, always using the language of tact and discretion, to his crude way of expressing himself—even Pano's French seemed to him marvelous, impeccable as his manners, in contrast to his own faulty French.

Alex had quickly struck up a friendship with this boy. Though they were years apart—Alex was only twelve to Pano's eighteen—they had many of the same tastes. They liked to shoot down birds over the lake and jump in after them with a shrill whoop of delight; they enjoyed swimming naked in the translucent waters and sleeping on the warm sand under the open sky, where they could study the star configurations that determine the fate of men. Their own horoscopes boded only well in those glorious spring days when the spacious, quiet mansion resonated with their laughter. They sat out on the portico overlooking a garden abloom with poppies and anemones, following their dancing movements over sunlit stones, listening to the cooing of the doves on the rooftop, and inhaling the sweet whiffs of fresh-baked *ghorayebah* cookies emanating from the kitchen. In this way, sunnily, delightfully, the days succeeded one another until one morning the big shadow of Pano's father cut across the portico, wrenching them out of their dreams: he had come to announce that he had decided to move his family to Australia.

In my mind's eye, I could see Alex sitting out on that portico long after his friend had gone to bed, listening dejectedly to the deep boom of the ships bound for distant lands—a sound like a death knell for someone like him, with no place to go.

When the *Queen Elizabeth* was due to sail, Alex told

me, he had gone to bid his friend farewell. He had stood there on the wharf, waving his white handkerchief, and had listened to the siren as the ship prepared to pull out of the harbor, which sounded to him like a long, sad wail. He had not cried, he said, because his family was there with him: he had just felt very faint when the boat gave out that last terrible, loud blast, which could be heard all over the port of Alexandria. And the tears had trembled on his lashes, making it even harder for him to discern the scarcely visible, motionless shape of his friend, leaning over the rails. Alex knew his friend was watching him. And so he stayed until the ship was swallowed up by the night, until from the ends of the earth, from all directions, came the pain. It bowled him over, buried him: for two years he ceased to exist outside that pain.

Thus we would summon back into our presence the old times that were all too rapidly fading, receding from us like pale stars on the horizon. For despite the revolution of 1952, Alex and I continued to "belong" to our different classes but to inhabit the same nation—that of the ancien régime. It was made up of fragments of the mosaic of languages and nationalities that had characterized the

Egypt of my early childhood. In my family circle, Egyptians, Syro-Lebanese, Italians, Greeks, Armenians, British, French, Muslims, Christians, and Jews had intermingled and intermarried. (Though the Egyptianization of the economy began in earnest in 1936, with the treaty of independence from Great Britain, the mass emigration of the foreigners who had developed, dominated, and depredated the nation's commerce and finance did not take place until the "socialist" decrees of the 1960s that targeted all the major industries, banks, and businesses. The age-old community of sixty thousand Greeks rapidly dwindled: those with money fled Nasser's "socialism" for the shores of North America and Australia, leaving behind their less fortunate brethren—low-ranking salesmen, craftsmen, and skilled workers.)

The native *masakin*, the poor, existed only as a backdrop to my family's splendid, cosmopolitan life. If we noticed them at all, it was at best with pity, at worst with disgust and fear. Theirs was a world we hardly knew outside of the organ grinders who came to beg for money under our windows. Father would toss them a coin, in exchange for which their monkeys would perform a few grateful somersaults. And Mother would shake her head, saying, "*C'est une honte! Le gouvernement devrait ramasser ces espèces et les mettre hors de vue.*" (It's a shame! The government should gather up these creatures and put them out of sight.)

Alexandria, the Alexandria of my childhood, was even further removed from this Egypt of rags and sores. Unlike Cairo, where Arabic was spoken, Alexandria had Italian, Greek, Armenian, Yiddish, and above all French—not Arabic—as its modes of exchange, and its atmosphere, manners, and social graces were those of Europe. It was to this Alexandria that Alex and I returned again and again in our conversations, compulsively, like a finger to a scab. Alex was a true child of this city, which was neither Egyptian nor European but a hybrid.

I, too, would become loquacious under the influence of a few beers: I would tell Alex about my school in Alexandria, the English Girls College, about myself, about my Italian friend Anna Cohen.

At fourteen, I was scrawny, with short dark brown hair and bangs, rather tomboyish in appearance. My mother's friends often commented on my green eyes; they said they were my prettiest feature. I took that to mean there was nothing else pretty about me. I envied my Italian friend Anna, her long silky mane of red hair and her breasts, which were larger than mine (I still had a child's flat chest). I wondered if she let boys touch them. She had always been precocious, immodest, too, even when she was small. She could have been no more than eleven when she came tearing out of the bathroom one night, chanting, "I have a hair on my wee-wee. I have a hair on my wee-wee," as she danced up and down the rows of our dormitory beds. Barely a year later, she was parading her burgeoning breasts throughout the boarding school. She never made use of the small cubicles at gym time, the way we did; she stood there and took off her clothes, smack in front of you. The girls didn't like the way she walked about naked; it just wasn't done. They jeered at her plump, pubescent body behind her back.

She was only thirteen, but already men looked at her in the street, and when we went to the movies, boys from Victoria College, our rival (the Victorians called us the English Gorilla Company and we referred to them as the Viper Club), offered her bouquets of roses. One of them, the son of a pasha rumored to be fabulously wealthy (his father had an entire room set up with electric toy trains for him when he was only seven), sent a big black Cadillac with a gloved chauffeur in full livery to wait for her every day after school. No one was quite sure where he took her, but the girls whispered that she had been *trouée*—"popped." Their heartless gossip notwithstanding, I was jealous of my friend's freedom. At school it was better to be an Italian-Egyptian, a Greek-Egyptian, an Armenian-Egyptian, a Syro-Lebanese–Egyptian, an Egyptian Jew—in short, any form of hyphenated Egyptian—than to belong to the majority of so-called native Egyptians to which I had the misfortune to belong. We were not allowed to go out with our boyfriends; we could go out only with a school group.

Yet we were better off than when my mother was a boarder. Mother and her sisters were not allowed out at all: indeed, her father was considered inordinately broad-minded for allowing his daughters to go off to school in the distant city of Cairo. In those days, it used to be said of a "nice girl" that she left her house only twice: once, after she was married, to transfer from her father's house to her husband's house, and once, when she died, to transfer from her husband's house to the family crypt. Mother's only diversion on Sundays was climbing up to the school roof to watch the people on the street below. Even that was more freedom than she was allowed at home. Once when her father caught her looking out her bedroom window, he lectured her severely on the dishonor that would befall the family if someone saw her. "But, Father, there is no one, the garden is empty," she protested. "No one, indeed! And our gardeners, aren't they men?"

Mother and her many sisters and female cousins were guarded jealously by Dada ("Nanny") Safran and Dada Morgan, the chief harem eunuchs, castrated male slaves who, even after being freed at the end of the nineteenth century, remained in the family for two generations. They had permission to beat the girls for any breach of conduct. They were the terror of everyone.

Mother claimed still to have the taste of salty tears in her mouth and still to hear the loud smacks administered by strong black hands to her quivering white bottom. "*Beyda zey el amar*" (white as the moon), Dada Safran used to say as he bathed my mother, his teeth flashing against his thick charcoal lips, like a black panther contemplating his prey approvingly. And he would laughingly pinch Mother's creamy, plump *derrière*, predicting an early marriage for her. Mother ardently hoped Dada's prediction would prove right. She had scribbled on her school locker: "*Mon Dieu, envoyez-moi un bon mari pour me délivrer de la tyrannie de mon père!*" (Dear God, send me a good husband to deliver me from the tyranny of my father!)

Mother's family was fabulously wealthy; they owned

some of the finest mango plantations in the Delta. In the book *Veiled Mysteries of Egypt*, S. Leeder, an Englishman visiting their estate in 1912, described it as follows: "I was not prepared for such a vision of cultivated beauty as burst upon us as soon as we passed through the gate in the high wall . . . Wealth alone could not have done it. Although wealth could bring treasures of fruit and flowers from the earth, it could not make them grow as they grow here." Within this "place of Elysian delight," however, the peasants lived in direst poverty, utterly at the mercy of their landlords, who made the laws and had virtual power of life or death over them. They could be lynched for so much as setting eyes on the landlord's daughter. When Mother and her sisters visited their estates in the village of Ishnawai, adjacent to the provincial city of Tanta where they lived, all the peasants had to drop their plows and turn their backs to the passing vehicle in order not to soil the girls with their eyes, even though the blinds had been drawn and the girls wore veils.

While I had told Alex a great deal about my family, I had never succeeded in finding out much about his. The once or twice I had tried to question him about his childhood, he had evaded the subject with a curious look of anxiety and distress. I had dropped it thereafter; I did not want him to feel I was prying into that which he wished to keep to himself.

Subjects about which it was fruitless to question him too closely: his age, his origins. I had put his age at the mid-thirties, and I surmised from Mother's description of the squalid little apartment in which she had found him that his family must have been poor, that he must have grown up in a similar cramped, noisy downtown European quarter in Alexandria, with a multitude of tiny workshops and garages situated at the bottom of broken, run-down buildings and of warehouses that were a breeding ground for rats, a quarter of swarming cafés and cockroach-infested apartments inhabited by Greeks, Armenians, Italians, White Russians, and East Europeans—communities cut off from their parents' body, by wars, deportations, and massacres, as abruptly and irrevocably as the branches of a tree struck down by a tornado. They raised their children on curses—in every conceivable language—and on blows, on stale pieces of Arab bread leavened with tears, on the compost odors of urine and mouse pellets in the open drains that served them as toilets, on long hours of hard work done at night, in the dim light of oil lamps, in homes turned into makeshift sweatshops for tailoring, carpentering, and printing. It was surely a quarter very different from the one where we resided, with its Sporting Club surrounded by the very English boxwood hedges and its jacaranda-lined avenues (George Lloyd, the British High Commissioner for Egypt, reportedly told an aide that whenever he saw the jacarandas in bloom, in the spring, he knew it was time to send for the battleships: the fragrance of their blue blossoms had an unsettling effect on the natives, inciting them to acts of violence).

The speed with which Alex had moved from one job to another before gaining employment in our household was staggering; it seemed to lend credence to the image I had of his deprived boyhood. Among other things, he had been a salesman in a Greek liquor store; a receptionist at a seedy little Greek pension called the Hotel Apollo; an orderly who gave injections under the auspices of St. Joseph's, an Italian religious order; and a masseur. He was a young man whose ambition had always been just that much greater than his ability to achieve. Yet he had not given up spinning projects that would turn him overnight into a millionaire, and he was never as talkative and as candid as when he dwelt on the details of such a project or drew pictures of what he would do with his first million. These pictures always entailed something bourgeois, smug, and orderly: a villa with silverware in proper rows, neat front lawns, and a shiny new car in the driveway. When he waxed lyrical over such things, I was reminded once more how immensely fortunate it was that he was so handsome. I could not otherwise have brought myself to listen to him.

But he was not always so garrulous. There were times when his sense of deprivation was so acute, his conviction that he had been cheated out of everything he had ever wanted in life so bitter, that he lapsed into a state of melancholic paralysis. A sort of suffering silence remained his only answer to my questions or solicitude.

Mother was convinced the only reason I was so taken with Alex was that I believed him to be secretly unhappy. She thought that as a "writer" I liked to cultivate a little "fashionable" unhappiness. Hence she reacted to my "infatuation" with him as she would have to a passing malady. But I was far from being anywhere near the end of my breathless enthusiasm for Alex. For even if I had to admit to myself that he was nothing so much as a shameless philistine, still his life illustrated for me a kind of plebeian passion, a pluck that I could only admire. He seemed to me in that phase of my life the most original person I had ever encountered, the most amusing, the most delightful to be with.

3

WHITE AS BUFFALO CREAM

ALEX'S DREAMS of success never encompassed others; his deprivation had not stirred in him any impetus toward social criticism. He would have laughed with derision if I had confessed to him that some of the stories of his life moved me, made me feel that true success must surely lie in my abandoning the haunts of the aristocracy and doing something for the suffering millions. He had no such ideals about uplifting the Egyptian masses; he simply loathed *les Noirauds* (the dark-skinned natives) because they were dirty and ignorant, with the outspoken violence of one who had known poverty.

From the outset, he had insisted on the distinction of being white—a distinction that earned him, among other things, the privilege of having his meals served to him separately in the dining room, instead of his having to eat with the rest of the staff in the kitchen. He liked to lord it over them, and the moment he was in their presence his bearing took on an artificial swagger, the swagger of the white man at large. He provoked them by stirring his contempt slowly, the way one would good Turkish coffee, as he observed them at work, saying scornfully that this, that, or the other thing was "typical" of Egyptians, or shaking his head and adopting a brooding attitude while he stood over them, weighed down by the White Man's Burden.

Not surprisingly, the servants responded to this with hostility. They had always mistrusted the *Khawaga* (foreign mister) who, by arriving in their midst, confirmed their inferiority and threatened their security. A white servant was for them an anomaly: in their view, a white man could only be a boss. Since Alex was not one of them, he was bound to be against them—a sort of family spy. So they thought it prudent to stop complaining about us in front of him: which one of them, they wondered, would end up losing his job on account of this white boy with the lordly manners of a *sayyid* (master)?

Alex's remarks were at times unabashedly racist: he once told me he never went to bed with natives because they were unclean. And another time, when we were watching a television broadcast of the visit of the Sudanese Prime Minister to Egypt, he remarked, with a snicker, that that *barbari* ("barbarian," a pejorative Arabic word for a Negro) would make a fine butler for our house.

If I was not as shocked at first by Alex's racism as I ought to have been, it was because it had been rubbed into me, too, very early on, that there was something superior about whiteness, something cleaner, purer, more refined, more distinguished—in short, infinitely more desirable. I had not forgotten how on returning home, aboard the *Esperia*, from the civilized shores of Europe, where we spent our summers, Father cringed at the sight of the puny, dark, kinky-haired men who swarmed like flies about the harbor where our ship had docked, bellowing, pushing, gesticulating, practically knocking the passengers down in their eagerness to carry their suitcases. How once he had turned to me and said, "*Shufi el bahayim di*" (look at these beasts of burden). In that one word *bahayim* was conveyed to me, at age eleven, the way we, the lighter-skinned members of the Turco-Egyptian aristocracy, looked at our less fortunate countrymen: as cattle, as a race without purpose or hope destined to replicate itself with frightful prolixity, like the street cats on our service stairs, and then, after a short life of brute labor, to vanish without leaving behind a single cultural artifact—nothing but the fly-infested mud hovels and filthy rags that were to serve its children as a future.

Had I not also noticed when I was little how when I went for walks with Father and we were pursued by hordes of beggar children calling out "*Khawaga, Khawaga*," he secretly exulted at being mistaken for a European, even though he pretended to be annoyed at them. Mother, too, beamed with pride when visitors, admiring my brother's blond curls, called him a little Englishman, even though she had spent half her life under the boot of the British occupier. And she never failed to remind me that I was lucky to be fair-complexioned, unlike my poor sister, whose true color showed beneath her layers of Caron powder.

I looked at my older cousins. Some of them, like my cousin Nadia, were very beautiful. Early on, I understood that her beauty was not due to her elegant clothes or to her expensive jewelry: it was due to her white skin. As with many other members of the Egyptian upper class, her color had been whitewashed through generations of intermarriage with Ottoman and European conquerors, as well as with Circassian concubines. "*Beyda zey el eishta*" (white as buffalo cream), the slave hawkers would call out; Circassian women, who had been imported from the Caucasus, fetched twice as much as the fine-featured, coffee-colored Abyssinians and three times more than the black slaves.

My own lineage was a typical example of this process of whitewashing. Grandfather first married a Frenchwoman he met in Paris, during his student days, and after her death a Turk, my grandmother. She was white-skinned, with a Rubenesque figure and a heavy mass of coppery hair. It was to her that my father and brother owed their blue eyes. Her ancestors hailed from Kavalla, a Macedonian port, from which the Ottoman fleet had set out to subjugate Egypt at the beginning of the nineteenth century. Her martial family name—"son of a cannon" in Turkish—was said to indicate her descent from a Balkan, who had been kidnapped at a time when it was still common practice to abduct little boys in the European provinces of the Ottoman Empire, convert them to Islam, and bring them up as soldiers in the Sultan's army.

My cousins took great care to preserve their white skin: their worst enemy was the sun. They guarded themselves against the sun as they would against a contagious disease: they never went out before dusk in the summer, and even then only in a car. They never walked. In the mornings, they idled about their large villas, drawing the venetian blinds down against the virulent sun, rubbing their faces with cucumber slices in order to lighten their complexions, attending to their manicures, trying on new dresses, looking at themselves in the mirror, dreaming of their future husbands. In the evenings, they visited one another; they sat outside on their breezy verandas and talked about skiing in St. Moritz, about the wonderful minigolf courses in Gstaad. Their conversations differed radically from those of the new class—though they both shared a dedication to trivia—because the nouveaux riches preferred to discuss their latest purchases: their VCRs, eleven-band radios, stereos, television satellites, or some other Japanese or American electronic marvel, and if they demonstrated any interest in the outside world that was not material in nature, it was mainly to show off their familiarity with the latest article in *Newsweek*, *Reader's Digest*, or the *Ladies' Home Journal*. (The Shakespeare collections in their plush new houses were false backs.) They differed also in that they were more comfortable speaking in Arabic. The old aristocracy chose to converse in English, because now English was the language of the young members of the upper crust, just as a generation earlier, French had been the language of polite Cairene society. But they interjected Arabic exclamations like *ma'lesh* (never mind), *mush ma'ul* (impossible!) and *ya'ni* (I mean to say) into their conversations. In fact, even Oxford-educated Egyptians with upper-class British accents would have been incapable of putting two simple English sentences together without availing themselves of the help of *ya'ni*.

My cousins were forever waiting, saving themselves: waiting for their summer vacations, saving themselves for their husbands-to-be. But I could not stand these long, hot days spent waiting. And long ago I had resolved not to go on saving myself.

4

THE REALM OF THE FORBIDDEN

IT WAS ONE of those torrid summer nights. I lay in the palpitating heat, thick with the rising vapors of the Nile, unable to sleep, listening to the voices emanating from the living room onto which my bedroom opened. (During the long hot months, we slept with our doors open, to create a draft.) Father, who was having another of his bouts of insomnia, sat up in his high-backed chair telling Alex how once, in Washington, D.C., when he had taken my sister to the Cinelux, which featured only newsreels, he was surprised to see himself on the screen delivering a speech to the UN

General Assembly, calling for the independence of Sudan from British rule and its unification with Egypt. To discredit the Egyptian claim to the Sudan (a claim based on the geographical unity of the Nile Valley), the British had juxtaposed a shot of my father, described as having an "air of indisputable refinement" and a "clipped British accent," with that of a half-naked black from the southern Sudan, dancing about frenetically to the clamor of drums. They had asked the viewers to judge for themselves if there was anything in common between the two men. This kind of anecdote always struck a responsive chord in Alex: he roared with laughter.

Indeed, there seemed no end to the conviviality next door. Father had launched into another of his delightful rambling monologues. He was now describing to Alex the estate of his friend the former British Ambassador to the United States, Lord Halifax, in Devon, with its rolling green lawns, its pony-driven wicker carts, and its cricket fields. The narrative rose in a steamy mist to envelop me: I listened on, lulled by his voice, until I heard what sounded like Father trying to lever himself out of his rattan chair, followed by a thud, indicating he had made a false start. There were some encouraging mutterings from Alex and then the sound of Father's shuffling footsteps and whimpering, panting breath.

After a longish wait, a persistent squeaking of Alex's chaise longue signaled his return. Was he making love to himself, I wondered. The first hint of my desire for him arose in that dark room, my nakedness close to his nakedness next door.

The next morning at table, our hands touched involuntarily. I had to fight so hard against my desire to place a kiss on his wrist that I felt myself turn red under his stare.

Until the day when, slipping under his mosquito net, I whispered to him, "*Engorge-moi*" (fill me), and he chased me away with a pillow, terrified lest Father should have overheard me, there had been nothing but teasing play between us. It had begun one morning when I had snatched out of his hand a snapshot that he was reluctant to show me because he claimed it made him look like an old goose with a wrinkled neck, and had run off with it down the corridor. My attempt to evade his pursuit was unsuccessful: I tripped and fell. He thrust himself upon me and tickled me to get me to release my grasp, and we lay thus for a long time, engaged in a contest of wills—one indistinguishable mass of writhing, helpless laughter. In the midst of this uproarious struggle, I thought I felt something hard against my thigh. This, too, he seemed to laugh off. We always laughed a great deal, Alex and I—laughed like two children. (I believe he was even then fonder of this hoyden who could outrun and outfight him than he liked to admit. As for me, I would certainly not have dreamed of characterizing the bewildering emotions he inspired in me at this stage of our relationship as love—though I definitely cared for him. I could not bear to hear him denigrated; it made me mad when my sister said to me, "*Il est aussi insignifiant qu'un pou*"—he's as insignificant as a louse.)

A few days after the snapshot incident, I stood before our Cerisier commode cutting off the heads of the petunias that were to float in a bowl of Bohemian crystal at lunchtime.

Alex snuck up behind me and pinched my nipples hard. When I swung around to him, a half-formulated reproach on my lips, he sealed them with a derisive kiss.

After that kiss, I would sometimes tease Alex by jumping up and down on my heels, behind Mother's back, in order to make my breasts bounce underneath my frock. I always chose to do it when one of my parents was in the room, because I knew he was dying to play with them and I derived a mischievous pleasure from the thought that it made his guard stand to attention behind his impassive air.

I like to remember that first kiss, a kiss broken off by his impudent laughter. It symbolized the passion we enjoyed—its humor and lightness.

On one of the most unromantic evenings imaginable, an evening of khamsin, hot desert winds, when every kiss tasted dusty, I crossed the bridge that connected Zamalik to the downtown area where Alex lived.

Two bridges linked our small island to the mainland. Kasr el Nil—"Palace of the Nile," named after Khedive Ismail's residence—the bridge our chauffeur took when driving me to school (my mother would not allow me to use public transportation for fear that *des gens sales*, the unwashed, would pass their germs to me by breathing in my face), led past the Sporting Club, whose scarlet-blossomed flame trees and red bougainvilleas grew defiantly alongside the neatly trimmed cricket fields. This club, of which my father was honorary president, had been built at the turn of the century for British officers and administrators and remained for a long time out of bounds to "wogs." My father was one of the first members of the Turco-Egyptian aristocracy "honored" with admission to it. When Nasser attempted to confiscate its polo fields to provide grounds for a youth club for the poor, Father resigned in protest. (Nasser backed down.)

The other bridge, Abou 'Ela, which our chauffeur had instructions to avoid, led to Bulak, the poor section of town, where Alex lived. Only on Sham el Nessim (literally, "inhaling the breeze"), a spring festivity dating back to the pharaohs, who celebrated it by sacrificing the fairest virgins to the Nile, were the poor brazen enough to cross over into our neighborhood. They invaded our riverbank: corpulent, middle-aged women in *malas* of crinkly dyed silk, heaving with effort as they balanced on their heads the big wicker baskets with the round loaves of brown bread, the green onions, and the *fessih*, a reeking pickled fish consumed on this occasion, which no upper-class persons would admit into their homes, as well as the *fitir meshaltit*, a country pie with molasses, while the men, who had nothing to carry, settled first along the narrow strip of grass, catching the hem of their striped galabias between their teeth as they sat down. Their children poured across the bridge clad in rakish cherry and orange tulles, the new frocks they had received for the occasion, and we would stand on the veranda, tittering and pointing fingers at their *baladi* clothes (an Arabic word, literally meaning "from the country," into which upper-class children are taught very early on to inject just the right amount of venom, so it would acquire the connotation of showy and cheap).

From their position on the bank of the Nile, they would look up at our apartment and observe our privileged life, rendered even more splendid by the dazzling light of our crystal chandeliers. And we would shudder a little at the thought of these invisible presences peering at us greedily out of the dark.

On those rare occasions when traffic jams at the intersection of the Kasr el Nil Bridge had compelled us to drive down the road where Alex lived toward the other bridge, I had been frightened by the ragged mobs that looked at us resentfully, unlike our complaisant servants: throngs of barefoot women converging on our car with outstretched palms—the runny nostrils of their sleeping infants beaded with flies—men with diseased eyes in keffiyehs; toothless, black-veiled hags; and naked little boys with bloated bellies. It was another nation, this downtown area with its raucous, dissonant music, its jabbing neon lights, its garishly painted portals, its insolently vulgar clothing, and, above all, its overwhelming odors. Even a left-wing upper-class Egyptian could not cross the Abou 'Ela Bridge without experiencing culture shock.

It had therefore taken me a long time to go to Alex's district. I had indeed walked once or twice in the direction of his house, but each time I had turned back as though what lay beyond was prohibited. It was not just my horror of Bulak that checked me—it was a kind of fear. Perhaps I understood that crossing over to his side of the river would mark a turning point in our relationship from which there would be no retreat. But once I had made up my mind to take the plunge, I threw myself into the murky waters with a vengeance, the way I always did when I was afraid of something—the more afraid I was of it, the more determined I was not to shrink from experiencing it.

And so one day I set out in search of his bachelor pad. I directed my steps down the narrow, fly-tormented lanes, where the reek of decomposing garbage mingled with that of hot pavements slaked with water, walking on sidewalks littered with vendors' trays, displaying copper hands against the evil eye, amulets, gilded medallions with the name of Allah, phosphorescent prayer beads and incense from Saudi Arabia, paper fans and spices from India, plastic thongs from Hong Kong, locally made combs and mirrors; past a bevy of giggling girls, in colorfully embroidered headcloths, who were rifling through secondhand magazines, laid out on the floor, while their owner sat on a burlap sack wiping his nose on his shirt sleeve; past an old woman fanning her incense burner at the entrance of a dark, decrepit building; past a man with greasy sideburns, scratching his crotch as he gaped up at the movie posters; past a modestly dressed mother whose long blue pants showed underneath her skirt. She was squatting on the curb, picking lice out of her daughter's hair with a lice comb, while, next to her, another mother was fishing out her breast from the side slit of her long flowery gown and pushing her taut purple nipple into her sleepy infant's mouth.

Young men in modern outfits—ill-cut bell-bottoms and loud ties—were peeling long strips of sugar cane with their teeth, masticating and spitting out the pulp as they dragged their lean, sulky bodies along the hot sidewalks. Their veiled wives, always at a respectful distance, were pushing their huge bellies in front of them and pulling a whole troop of toddlers behind them. There were the ubiquitous loafing street curs and self-mutilated beggars, pickpockets, magicians and fortune-tellers, and students in pajamas (a popular form of outdoor clothing in Egypt, because their material is subsidized by the government) who made a pretense of studying their soiled, tattered textbooks, while glancing sideways at the women in the tightly wrapped black *milayas*, who swung their fat buttocks as they walked, and jingled their *kholkhals* (ankle amulets).

A few predatory males, with leering eyes, were hanging about a gaily decorated *granita* (water-ice) cart. I asked where 33 Antiquity Street was, and the thick-browed Italian ice-cream vendor pointed in back of him to some bushes starred with white blossoms—jasmines.

I reached a garden gate that was off its hinges and walked past a citrus grove and flower beds ravaged by neglect, toward a four-story building with cracked, scaling walls. The elevator was out of order, so I made for the staircase, whose balustrade had intermittent missing spindles. It gave off an overwhelming smell of dust, but it was a sweet-smelling dust spiced with rotten fruit, stale jasmine, and human sweat. From the open window on the second-floor landing I gathered that the back yard served as a garbage dump, while the stranded elevator on the third floor was home to the neighborhood's stray cats.

Alex lived in the topmost apartment. His entrance, which was flanked on both sides by potted zinnias and snapdragons, gave onto a roof used for hanging laundry. I stood outside his door waiting for my pounding heart to quiet down. Then, taking a deep breath, I rang the bell.

He opened the door and started at the sight of me. "Did anyone see you?" he whispered. I began to reassure him, but without waiting for my reply he grabbed me by the elbow and pulled me inside. Veering around, he said to me curtly, "You shouldn't have come here. Please leave." I went and sat on his bed. Alex remained standing and, in the same dry tone of voice, reiterated impatiently, "You *must* leave."

I noticed that the cigarette was trembling in his hand and it dawned on me that he was afraid. He was afraid of being found out, fired. He didn't have the strength to love me in opposition to my family, to surmount the class difference.

I myself felt a twinge of fear: I remembered Dina. She was the head girl at the English Girls College. Tall, slender, very classy, with grave, almond-shaped eyes, she had a diffidence that passed in school for an enigmatic reserve. Like many of the small children in Lower IV Byron, I had a crush on her. I would put little packages of Bazooka bubble gum under her pillow, always accompanying my gift with an ardent billet-doux. Alas! she hardly noticed me: she was eighteen, in her last year of studies, earnestly preparing for her A-level exams in Upper VI Shakespeare, and she had a boyfriend, a young Englishman who taught arithmetic at the Scottish Boys School, across the street from us. She would wait up for him at night, after the house mistress had turned off the lights, looking fixedly out of the window at the mimosa trees down below. We all knew that he crept over the fence and that the moment she thought we had fallen asleep, she would steal away to her rendezvous in the school garden.

For a long time the dormitory went on reverberating with the sighs of my unrequited love for Dina. Then one day she vanished. We were told—and this was meant to be a lesson for the rest of us—that her father had found out about her secret meetings and had withdrawn her from school: he was planning to marry her off to his cousin, a rich, elderly village notable. The young Englishman was broken-hearted, but there was little he could do because the father wouldn't hear of his daughter marrying a man she had known before marriage—even though he had offered to convert to Islam—and his dreams of eloping with her crashed against the implacable rigidity of Egyptian law, which had always been hostile to the freedom of women: it stipulated that no woman be granted an exit visa, a requirement for leaving the country under Nasser, without her father's (or husband's) written permission. When Dina went on weeping and ended up slashing her wrists, on the eve of her wedding day, her father had her locked up in the insane asylum, under the pretext that she was hysterical, so she would never be able to set eyes on her boyfriend again.

Soon Dina was forgotten—but not by me. I often saw her in my mind's eye, being carted off by force in a white ambulance to the isolation hospital, much in the same way as I had witnessed, when I was very little, the street dogs being rounded up in the public park where I had been playing. Terrified, I had stood by and watched in silence as they were hauled away in a white van to be gassed. Dina's hospital was called Sarayet el Maganin, the palace of the madmen, by the common folk—and with good reason. In the depth of a shadowy garden, the British had erected an impressive, vaguely fin-de-siècle fortress; its grim façade was camouflaged by cypress and banyan trees. A place where people were buried alive, because therapy in Egypt had not progressed beyond the notion that disturbing elements ought to be weeded out of society, quarantined, left to themselves to die a slow death. Sometimes I thought of Dina's shrieks, her terrible fear at being surrounded by impassive white-frocked men armed with tranquilizing syringes, and at waking up later to find her hands and feet tied to the frames of the narrow gilt-iron bed, in a huge ward with an immaculate checkered white-and-black-tile floor, which smelt of formaldehyde—for her own good, the sister assured her, so she would not hurt herself. Sometimes I imagined her leaning against a tree, gazing straight ahead of her, alone, queenlike, in the hospital garden with the weeping tamarisks, where she was let out, every afternoon, in a straitjacket for her daily walk.

Dina. Stranded amid the weeping tamarisks, amid the checkered black-and-white-tile floors, amid the gilt-iron beds, amid madness. Dina, whose crime was love; condemned to a frightful loneliness, to fear, to oblivion.

But for now I chased away these chilling thoughts: I told Alex to come over, to possess me. He threw himself on me, shouted at me, beat me, called me a slut, a whore, until at last, worn out, he fell silent and lay perfectly immobile on the bed beside me with his eyes closed, as though he could contrive to banish me that way. Slowly, I explored his eyelids, mouth, hair with my lips. He stirred, his hands began to move over my body . . .

He struggled to undo my top, but his fingers, which were fumbling with the buttons at the back of my blouse, became entangled in the folds, and he began instead to tear desperately at my neckline. I drew my blouse up over my head, pulled him toward me, and buried his head in my ample breasts. I was proud of the abundance of this part of my body, which I had always regarded as just compensation for my physical shortcomings.

For a while, I lay back in passive contentment, letting Alex savor my nipples. But as his tongue began its descent toward my navel and his right hand traveled up between my thighs, I could contain myself no more. I wriggled out of his grasp, and we began a tug of war; the first round ended abruptly when he shuddered and fell limp with a moan. For a few minutes he lay in a virtual daze, panting and sweating as after a cavalry charge.

But our amorous match had only served to further inflame my passion. I tackled his ass, nibbling at it until a rosy tint suffused it. I chuckled with delight at the sight of it, for nothing was more rousing to me than those perfect, gently curving lobes, smooth, intoxicating in their whiteness, with the sheen of polished marble.

They triggered in me memories of earlier childhood pleasures. I could have been no more than seven or eight when I stood on tiptoe stroking and trying to rub myself up against Mother's generous posterior, as she leaned over the banister, talking to the maid at the bottom of the staircase. It felt wondrously soft, like the sumptuous satin pillows on her bedstead, which I liked to cuddle in my arms because they smelled of the essences with which she anointed her head and body. And what a delight it had always been to be allowed to share Mother's bed, when Father was away on business trips. How fragrant, how sweet, she seemed to me as I lay with my head resting against the pillows and my arm tightly wrapped around her waist. There was no one in the whole world who enjoyed a more blissful sleep than I.

My first sense of sexual shame, of a sudden loss of innocence, came to me in that villa in Alexandria when Mother, turning away angrily from the banister, frowned and said, "*Cesse! Ce n'est pas jolie ce que tu fais là*." (Stop it! What you're doing isn't at all nice.)

I was never again nearly so bold as I was on that first night with Alex, never quite so eager to take the initiative, never so spirited in my response. In no time at all, my amorous assaults had succeeded in rejuvenating his member, and I gave in to an access of passion, and mounted it.

At last we were spent. I collapsed in a virtual swoon onto his chest. For a long time we remained thus, our perspiring bodies glued to each other, listening to the rusty grating of the overhead fan, until, exhausted, we slept.

When I opened my eyes, Alex was standing before a small sink redolent of urine—he was too lazy to go down to the toilet on the second-floor landing—washing himself with deft, swift movements and gasping at the coldness of the water. It took me only one trip to the toilet to appreciate the advantage of that shortcut. I had to stand on two sole-shaped ledges and squat over a hole in the ground, for the only furnishing in the bathroom was a large bin into which used toilet paper was to be thrown because the old flush box did not work well. The bin overflowed with feces-smeared tissue paper, on which hordes of ravenous flies feasted. But the disgust it inspired in me was nothing by comparison to what I felt at the sudden surge of a battalion of huge, amber-colored cockroaches; they lumbered close by my feet, poised, waiting for that helpless moment to graze me with their feathery antennas. These repulsive apparitions, together with the suffocating heat of that little toilet and the stench, made emptying one's bowels a veritable ordeal. (Though Alex claimed one got used to it, it took a long time for me to be able to stifle my civilized instincts sufficiently to pay it another visit.)

Alex opened his soapy eyes and, noticing that I was sitting up observing him, wiped his face and came over to me with a cocky smile. Kneeling by the bed, he took my underlip between his small, fine teeth.

We dressed in silence and, furtively, like two accomplices, made our way down the dark, fetid staircase into the open street, from which emanated the ululations of a funeral procession. We walked without daring to link arms amid the blood-curdling cries of tearful black-garbed women, screaming, wailing, striking their chests, scratching their cheeks, past the Egyptian Museum of pharaonic and Greco-Roman antiquities, situated diagonally across from Alex's neighborhood, down to the taxicab stand in rue Champollion (a street named after a French savant who accompanied Napoleon to Egypt and deciphered the hieroglyphics on a stone discovered in the port of Rosetta). As we pushed and wriggled through the crowded lanes, a bunch of squalid shoeshine boys, who had been sitting listlessly on their boxes apparently without the energy to wave away the flies that crawled all over their faces, jumped up and began soliciting us.

"Let's go," I said to Alex, a trifle impatiently, for they smelt dreadful, those half-naked, sweat-larded children, with their grubby hands; and despite myself, I shrank at their touch. But I could see that Alex was not at all unnerved by their clinging to his legs with their skinny arms, wheedling and intoning, "*In Allah yuhib al mohsinin*" (Allah loves the doers of good deeds). He was at home in this strident native quarter with its insistent smells and sounds. He walked into the press of human beings, gazing about him with an affection born of familiarity, his nostrils drinking in the scent of sweat mingled with that of aromatic foods and spices, and his ears the barking of dogs; the curses of street urchins; the shrieks of the buyers of secondhand wares; the cries of hawkers; the endearments of harlots; the imprecations of pimps; the whispered solicitations of men in galabias peddling obscene pictures, girlie magazines, aphrodisiacs, infertility remedies, and other questionable merchandise freshly smuggled in from Port Said; the long sobbing calls of Muslim preachers. Alex bought from a street vendor a necklace of fresh jasmine for me and for his parrot a "lucky" mirror, so he would have the illusion of company. Everywhere he went, the cries of the street greeted him: *Naharak said, ya Khawaga.* (May your day be a happy one, *Khawaga.*) *Izay el hal, Khawaga?* (How are things, *Khawaga*?) And he responded radiantly. For he might have been poor, unknown, and full of ungratified aspirations, he might have had to work as an orderly in Zamalik and live on Antiquity Street amid belittered alleys, shabby interiors, and neighbors with soiled collars and personal odors, yet here among the disinherited natives his white skin made him a lord.

Seeing him in this locale, I understood for the first

time why he did not leave Egypt and seek out a new place where he would not be haunted by failure and a sense of deracination. There was more to him than just a youthful, brash male urge to thrust himself into prominence: there was a sentimental side. No matter how much he might have loathed the squalor and filth of this clamorous, clangorous city, he belonged here by adoption: he was an *ibn balad*—a native son. Once when I had caught sight of some mice frolicking underneath his sink and asked him why he didn't move to better living quarters, he had answered me with a shrug. "Why should I—they're my good neighbors!"

Alex had drawn his strength from Egypt's crowded streets and hustling traffic; he had endowed its shops, massage parlors, and hotels with his ambitions; he understood this country by instinct and loved and hated it with passion; he represented its vulgarities and curiosities, its cunning and impudence, but also its humor and good nature.

Alex lost his seductive aplomb the moment we stepped into a cab. He did not talk to me on the way home, did not look at me, did not even smile once. He dropped me off at the corner of my street, in front of the Park Lane building, and drove away without a word.

I left him with a sigh and prepared a new face to greet my parents. As I approached the house, I spotted my sister's tall, gaunt figure on the veranda. She seemed to stand, lurk, behind the darkness of the parapet, contemplating me with an air humorless and far too disapproving even for one who had never been young. For some time now she'd been watching us, Alex and me, watching us with that same cold, alert fury, as we went off happy, arm in arm, laughing for all we were worth every afternoon while Father napped, down to Groppi's to feast on ice cream flavored with pistachios and *mistika* (gum), Alex's favorite. She must have guessed what had just taken place between us, because, lately, having to deal with Father's incontinence had shed considerable light for her on those facts of life she had not had a chance to learn from experience.

It may easily be believed that it cost me a great deal to squeeze into the dangerous little space of Alex's apartment. But our friendship had no chance to develop within the parameters of my family's home. The only format my parents considered proper for social intercourse with Alex was that of master with servant. Even if my sister did not quite share this view, she nonetheless felt Alex should be confined to the periphery of our charmed circle of privileges. The one time I had asked her to include us in a social activity—she was giving an informal luncheon on the northern veranda for Prince Abbas Hilmi, the grandson of Khedive Abbas Hilmi, who had been exiled in 1914 by the British on account of his support for the nationalist cause, and I thought it would please Alex if we invited his cousin, then on a visit from Greece, along with the cousin's friend Olympia, the Greek owner of Hotel Apollo, of whom he was quite fond—my sister sneered, exclaiming, "*Mais tu plaisantes, ma parole! Elles ont l'air d'être des vendeuses chez Groppi*" (You must be joking! They look like salesgirls at Groppi's). As for my parents, they considered the fact that I now wanted to invite "Greek grocers" (our district boasted of two of the finest Greek groceries, Vasilakes and Thomas, so for them all the Greeks were grocers) as just another of my eccentricities. They kidded about it between themselves, and while they were prepared to tolerate my excesses as private vagaries, they did not care for them to be made public.

Precisely because my association with Alex was confined, restricted, pressed in on, the only refuge left to me was his apartment. Anywhere else, in a café, club, or bar, we were subjected to stage-whisper comments and curious stares. Even the cinema was out of bounds because we might run into a relative and risk a nasty scene. The only possibility of privacy was going to see an Egyptian film, which no one of the upper class would deign to go to, but that would have meant having to sit through an endless tear-jerking saga, yawning, sweating, and getting bitten by fleas. And later, when the cinema disgorged its crowds, having to deal with the kinky, oily-haired hoods who swerved to brush their excited members against me and called out coarse remarks.

5

SECRETS

WHEN WE WERE NOT out together, Alex was very secretive about his whereabouts. I had to fight very hard against my desire to intrude upon the hidden side of his life. He seemed to have no friends outside of a Danish architect who lived in Old Cairo near the Khan el Khalili bazaar and studied *sabils*, medieval Islamic water fountains, and whom he occasionally brought home for drinks. A slender, graceful young man with an air of smiling diffidence, he struck me as perfectly charming. Soft-spoken and gentle-mannered, he had brought some of that gentleness to bear on the very real unhappiness of Alex's life.

The only other person I had seen with him was a dumpy, elderly woman, whom I once admitted into our salon, muffled from head to toe in a *milaya*, one of those black satiny sheets worn by lower-class Egyptians out of modesty, to conceal their charms. When I returned with Alex and she lifted her crumpled, fat body out of the Louis Quinze armchair, turning on him her flaccid face with eyes of a faded honey color, he seemed distinctly displeased to see her. She in turn looked at him in a manner so bewildered and wounded as to make me wonder what was afoot.

The next morning I said to him, "Who was that woman who came to see you yesterday?" His breath seemed to fail him for a moment. "What woman?" Poor Alex! He staged a gallant fight to recover his former nonchalance, and then, "Oh! *that* woman. She's a dressmaker," he offered, smiling snootily as he uttered that word, as though at the thought of her pathetic, limited life, of the patient, modest effort of her needle and thread. When I wondered why she had come to see him, he came back with a story about a vest she had mended for him. I sensed there was more than he let on, but for the time being I was content to let the matter rest.

I spotted the woman a couple more times after that incident, at the threshold of our house, always with that same forbearing, placid face, always carrying a small bundle under her arm. Alex invariably planted himself in the doorway as an impenetrable barrier, and remained there for the whole span of her visit, seemingly determined to deny her entrance.

Was he dealing in secondhand clothes to make an extra pound or two on the side, or in smuggled goods, I wondered. But I could only speculate, for he had none of that effusive confidence characteristic of Mediterraneans, who don't mind chatting freely about themselves.

In this manner I went on bumping into his hidden past. From his Greek cousin, who had moved to Athens after her Egyptian husband died but who returned to Egypt now and then to look after her property, I learned that Alex had suffered for years from some liver ailment, which she attributed to his having eaten too many cakes when he was a boy. He had a terrible sweet tooth, she told me. She had once discovered him lying ill in his dingy little apartment, after he had gorged himself on an entire kilo of mangoes. She had scolded him as one would a little boy, telling him that if he did not learn to stick with a job he would end his days thrown into the poor ward of some hospital, where he'd be left to die like a street dog without anyone to bring him so much as a bowl of soup. This chilling admonition had apparently served to press him into our service, though he had begged her not to let on that he was an orderly in our house, lest people suppose him responsible for such undignified tasks as wiping the Pasha's eminent bottom. She was to say instead that he was *le secrétaire du pacha*.

I liked to tell myself that I began to spy on Alex more out of disinterested curiosity than out of jealousy. At any rate, my jealousy, with its inconsistencies, its denials, its illogical machinations—and even a certain daredevil humor that played through it—amused him, and he led me on. One Sunday, however, as I moped about the house, disconsolate at the prospect of having to spend yet another day without him, one of my spies brought me the heartening news that the woman named Cyma whom he had gone to see—and who had caused me many sleepless nights—was no more than an old Armenian fortune-teller. (His faith in a fortune-teller did not surprise me: nothing characterized Alex so much as a morbid superstition. If anyone was so ill advised as to pay him a compliment, he would respond—much to the person's surprise—by lunging forward, fingers pointed in a V sign, to poke out the offender's eyes, by crossing himself vigorously, and by making the Arab motion of spitting on the ground. Warding off the evil eye required this elaborate ritual, he assured me.)

Thereafter my spies brought me only fragmentary and uninteresting information. Then one day in the sultry heat of a midsummer afternoon, stuck in a traffic jam in the heart of Cairo, I unexpectedly caught sight of Alex, his hair looking very blond against his blood-red shirt, trying to shake off a troop of mocking teenage girls, who followed close on his heels, swaying their hips back and forth.

All of a sudden I realized what was going on and reached out to lower the windowpane, noticing in an objective, detached sort of way how sweaty my palms felt as I did. But before I had time to call out his name, the traffic jam cleared and the cab pulled out of Soliman Pasha Square (a square named after a French officer, Colonel Sève, who chose to stay on in Egypt after Napoleon's defeat and converted to Islam).

I brooded over this baffling and disturbing scene, taking myself for a long walk along the riverbank, a prey to sharp doubts, suspicions, and fears. But I did not dare ask him for an explanation when I returned home lest he accuse me of spying on him.

Sometime later, my sister's Greek mechanic came to

deliver her repaired car, and spotting Alex placing in Wedgwood bowls the jasmine petals with which he liked to perfume our bedrooms at dusk to make the heat more bearable, he asked me how long Alex had been in our employ. He then proceeded to tell me he knew Alex "well," with an insinuating smile I did not care for. When I questioned him, he volunteered the information that they had been together in the Greek school in Alexandria and that Alex had been kicked out at the age of thirteen because he was discovered in the lavatory with an older boy.

Stupefied by this calamitous information, I went about the house like a sleepwalker for days, hardly conscious of my surroundings. My talent for surmounting challenging predicaments, which had served me so well in my erratic bohemian life, proved singularly absent. One night, unable to endure this torment any longer, I confided to Alex that I had run into an old school chum of his. The smile on his lips suddenly expired; something halfway between doubt and apprehension played about his eyes.

"And what did he tell you?" he said, smiling thinly.

"Aha!" I replied, raising a teasing eyebrow.

My remark enraged him. He stomped out of the room. When I caught up with him, he turned on me with a look of savage defiance and yelled, "He told you I was an orphan, didn't he?"

Speechless with surprise, I could not bring myself to answer right away. After regaining my composure, I asked him what on earth had put such a weird notion into his head. Besides, it was no great shame to be an orphan, I added. Then I told him what the mechanic had said, repeating the very same sentences, the same bold, naked, outrageous words.

I heard a muffled cry, and before I had time to check him, his hand swung across my face. In this strange and frightening experience, I caught a glimpse for a moment of the other Alex—the one who had always eluded me.

I ruminated over his outburst. He had not denied a single word. Yet for a long time I remained with the same aghast, indignant unbelief I had experienced when I finally comprehended what the mechanic meant.

One day, as Alex sat cross-legged on his bed, shuffling his tarot cards with those slender hands with the delicate wrists—on the back of which it was almost a shock to discover a few coarse hairs—and frowning as though he detected an ominous turn in his fortune, he began narrating his life history to me. He described to me, nostalgically, his Alexandrian boyhood.

In the Alexandria of those days, everything was yours for the asking, if you were young—the sea, the sun-kissed beaches, the hibiscus-rimmed balconies with identical weather-beaten green shades that ran all the way down to the small harbor, the outdoor cinemas where you held hands in the dark, the cheek-to-cheek dances. There Alex had been able to find a way of life commensurate with his beauty. But at the age of sixteen his pampered youth had been cut short by his mother's untimely death.

Alex's father, it seemed, had not been nearly so poor as I had imagined. He was in fact the well-to-do owner of a whole chain of pastry shops and movie theaters; Alex referred to him as *un sale type*, a cad, telling me wryly that he had promptly married a mistress ("before my mother had turned cold in her grave"). This *vipère* had then spared no effort to poison his father's mind, pointing out that Alex neglected the *pâtisserie* and took money out of the register to spend on good times with his friends. Alex had always wanted to be a dancer, but his father, who thought ballet was for sissies, insisted that being a cashier would be excellent preparation for his future as the manager of the family business.

One day his stepmother discovered a makeup kit in Alex's closet and called his father to come look at the "girl he had sired." He was so revolted by the discovery that he threw Alex out of the house on the spot. And at the prodding of his wife, he later proceeded to disinherit him. "She had finally gotten what she wanted, the . . . !" Alex exclaimed, punctuating his remark with an unprintable Greek word. After a moment's reflection, he added in a tone of incongruous cheerfulness, "But God avenged me. My father died of cancer," and went on to say that his stepmother wasn't able to enjoy his share of the inheritance for long. Shortly after his father died, she herself had succumbed to a horrible disease, he proclaimed with gloating delight.

These moods of vengeance and bitterness would sometimes be triggered by the appearance of the name of one of his father's relatives in an obituary in the *Journal d'Egypte*. He would turn away from the paper as if to prove to himself that he could ignore those who had been ashamed of him as completely as they had ignored him. But he would then proceed to sit up all through the night with a sullen expression on his face, shuffling and reshuffling his soiled, dog-eared pack of tarot cards and cursing under his breath in Greek. It was pointless to try and talk to him; there was no way to draw a single syllable from him. Nor could I persuade him that the cards could in no way influence his future; he had nothing but contempt for my kind of rationality, which, as he saw it, belonged to the phony Western world of science and illusion. He did not know when or how the calamity foretold by his cards would afflict him—he had long ago abandoned the hope of understanding such things through rational examination—but he considered it an ineluctable event. He was convinced that there was a curse on his family and that God himself was seeing to the execution of its terms. Hence Alex's frequent bouts of devotion, his fervent nightly prayers before the icons of the Virgin by his bedside, and his loud bargaining with the many saints who now populated our living room walls.

It was a measure of his growing hold on my family that Father found nothing objectionable about having his own glorified pictures flanked by those of smiling St. Lucy, whose eyeballs were missing on account of her faith, and St. Elmo, whose two-meter-long intestine was being wrenched out of his open gut while he contemplated his tormentor with an air of benign sorrow. Prolonged meditation before these pictures seemed to change Alex's outlook from one of passive hopelessness to a conviction that all obstacles could be surmounted through a tenacious faith in Christ.

On such nights he never went to sleep without reciting as many prayers as he could remember from his childhood to ward off impending calamities.

These were not the only occasions on which I noticed that Alex was a stickler for religious observance: on Sundays we would often begin our day together with a visit to the Protestant church. Though Alex was Greek Orthodox, he happened to like the Swiss pastor in charge of that congregation, whose long, dull, stern exhortations and grim evocations of the torments of hell elicited great enthusiasm from him. After the sermon, Alex would leave with his head proudly erect, his fine face ennobled by the publicness of his virtue. My own atheism exasperated him. He told me more than once that I would surely be damned to hell for the wickedness of my opinions.

Of all the contradictions of Alex's character, this religiosity struck me as the most curious. Once when I expressed some skepticism before one of his recurrent bouts of religious devotion, he cried out irritably, "You don't understand! I don't believe in God. I'm afraid of him."

If he placed his faith in Christ for the improvement of his lot, he also adhered fiercely to the creed that his white skin was his salvation: it would sooner or later magically transform his life, even if he was currently down and out. He clung to his whiteness the way one might to armor, clung to it with a passionate belief that it made him the equal of the most high-born Egyptian. However critical he was of his father, who had been willing to let him "croak in a hole," he had to admit that he at least owed him this one precious gift. When he recognized that, his heart softened a little and he would say he did not hate his father quite as much as he might be expected to under the circumstances, because the man had expiated his wrongs through his final agony.

It took some time for it to sink in that Alex's white skin meant nothing in our milieu, because he lived on the wrong side of the river. I don't know exactly when this first dawned on him. It might have been when we went shopping together on the 26th of July Street and he noticed how the rich people from our neighborhood pushed past him and called on the salesman who was attending to him. And how the salesman immediately dropped him and turned to the fancy dame in the mink coat, and when she had left and he reluctantly came back to Alex, he had managed to forget what it was that

Alex had asked him for. Or perhaps it was when I had tried to take him with me to the Sporting Club. He had been stopped at the gate. He pretended not to give a damn. Yet I am sure he must have felt a terrible longing to be allowed in, to become a part of the world of the club, where the leisure class gathered. He needed the club as badly as they needed the club, its recreation facilities, its black *soufragis*, in their snowy-white turbans, who served drinks to the men reclining on shaded deck chairs, opposite the cricket fields, while they watched the girls stretch out under the softly swaying parasols, their little breasts jiggling inside their clinging woollen jump suits—all those things, in short, that are needed to bolster one's ego and protect one's sanity if one has to live in a third-world country like Egypt. I could tell as we walked past the polo grounds that a terrible drama was taking place privately: he wanted to mount every horse, to play every golf hole, to hand out baksheesh right and left to the caddies, as nonchalantly as the jauntily dressed young man in the nifty blue shirt, whose starched cuffs rattled briskly against his worsted pants, was doing—all of which made him smart with the recognition that he belonged to a class whom the Cairene upper crust didn't so much as deign to rest their eyes on for half a second. By now he had become accustomed to the way the rich looked right through him, but still more time would be needed for that realization to give birth to yet another: the idea that his father had succeeded in making him nothing, nothing.

Sometime around then I had begun to feel that Alex was mine and I his—even though he still had it in his head that he had not a single friend in the immense, egotistical, indifferent world of Cairo, which defied him and mocked his poverty. His vulgar vitality, the disparity between the grace of his physique and his coarseness, had ended up making him indispensable to me. He might be irritating, even exasperating at times, but he was never boring. His salacious gossip and amusing stories, his outrageous opinions and shrewd perceptions, his bad grammar and charming French accent were now all part of my enchanted little world. It was just as he was, superficial or profound, that he held me.

Pretty soon an existence without him began to appear to me so boring as to be insupportable. His street life seemed much more appealing than my tedious home life. I waited impatiently for him to come home to give me an account of some new conquest: of the tall blond German tourist, a gorgeous stud he had met in the small, ramshackle booth by the bus station, with the barrel-shaped tin urinals that were emptied daily, who had slipped his arm around Alex's shoulder and, without further formalities, escorted him to a hotel bedroom; of the dimpled American sailor with the crocodile tattoo, who had drawn him behind a bush on the consulate grounds, of his enormous penis, rigid as an obelisk, and his hefty thrusts, which made the palm tree shake. Alex seemed to envelop everyone he met in a kind of spell—even women. For though he may have had a sort of feminine fragility, there was something dark and ambiguous about his nature that women found disturbing. And perhaps his attraction for women had also something to do with his highly developed and very male self-assurance, which led him always to expect to have his way.

At times, to be sure, when I watched Alex croon over some piece of jewelry he had received as payment for his services, I was filled with disgust for him—almost loathing. He told me these gold tidbits were given to him by an ugly Syrian, *un vieux crapaud* (an old toad) to whose house he repaired weekly, ostensibly to massage the man's arthritic knee, so his wife would not suspect anything. I had on occasion spotted the Syrian's black Mercedes nosing along the corniche in front of our house, but Alex had never brought him upstairs. Then one night, when I was having a drink with a friend at the Four Corners, he entered with Alex. I observed him leisurely, without being seen, from my corner table behind the arabesque screen. He was a short, squat, heavy-set man with a blotchy complexion and pendulous scarlet ears, showily dressed in a Hawaiian shirt open to the waist. I noted the little gold cross that nestled on his chest, amid the thick tufts of kinky black hair, coarse as a porcupine's. Alex sat with his back to me. I saw him laugh with the Syrian, saw him shaking his head vigorously, saw him drinking heavily despite his liver condition. Then they got up to leave. I held my breath as Alex passed by; he was so close to me for a moment that I could distinguish his citrus scent amid the clouds of other perfumes in the room.

Next morning, when I expressed disapproval, he lashed out in fury: "You speak as though I have a choice. What did you expect a poor devil like me, buried in a squalid corner of Cairo under a million stupid natives, to do? I had no family name, no money, no *wasta* [an Arabic word for influential connections] like you!" Then he went on to assure me that it was not the Syrian's money that interested him; it was the prospect that the man would use his influence to help him advance in life. In the same breath he avowed that he hung about the Syrian not for the advantages to be gained from being patronized by a rich man but simply for the thrill of a new experience.

The next time I caught sight of the Syrian—five feet by four of gristle and bristle, he was talking to Alex in the darkened embrasure of our doorway—I waited for Alex to notice me and introduce us, but his face remained blank, absolutely impenetrable beneath his cocked fedora. The Syrian's soft, large, bulging eyes brushed me for a moment, and he saluted me with a florid gesture. The hairy, chubby little hand he extended toward me, the way he oozed charm from every pore, accompanying his lingering handshake with that deep-voiced Mediterranean casuistry, made me shrink.

Thereafter I could not bear the thought of his gross intimacies with Alex. But I stopped moralizing: it was pointless. Alex responded irritably to the examples I gave him of this or that person we knew who had managed to succeed by dint of hard, honest work. His own observations of society had not been such as to impress him with its high moral tone, and sometimes I could not help but find his cynicism persuasive. He had far more experience than I, having been schooled in Cairo's devious alleys, and he often tried to shock me with stories of what he had observed in the back rooms and bars of the establishments where he had been compelled to work. Pretty soon he had managed to convince me that many of these "bourgeois types" who moved in my family circle were hypocrites, and, in this regard, he had as low an opinion of his own kin as he had of the natives.

Alex never wore the bracelets and rings that the Syrian had given him, but he seemed to derive some kind of sordid satisfaction from frequently taking his booty out of his small chest to polish it and contemplate it.

The sight of him holding it this way and that in the light, above the mirror of the chiffonier, to better examine it, admiring the reflection of the blue beads against the evil eye, the ankh, and other cheap amulets that dangled from his slender wrist, had the effect of qualifying my affection for him, and I would find myself toying with the thought of ending our relationship. But when, turning away from his self-worship, he would cast a coy smile in my direction, I would feel my resolution collapse. All at once I had nothing but pity and tenderness for his mediocrity: I had begun to find these gestures, these small vanities, which earlier seemed beneath contempt, charming. To be sure, it maddened me to think that he would sell himself to someone like the Syrian, yet I knew that I was incapable of imparting to him the sense of self-worth that had so long been denied him, and perhaps his weakness was all too familiar to me.

Trying to gain some insight into Alex's conduct, I frequently recalled to memory one of my uncles, a fat, bald man with a large nose surmounted by an impressive wart. When I was eight, he must have been in his seventies. Since he suffered from rheumatism, he was often in Badgastein during the summer at the same time as my family.

Whenever we entered the hotel dining room, Father, who was ashamed to sit next to my uncle because he slurped his soup and belched unabashedly, would whisper into my ear that I should pretend not to see him. Uncle's girth was so enormous that even though he docilely submitted to his wife's directives and stuck his napkin into his neckline, he never quite succeeded in covering his paunch completely. He always ended up being scolded by her for soiling himself, at which Father would mutter indignantly, "*Vraiment, quand on est gros comme ça, il ne faut pas manger du potage; c'est de l'inconscience!*" (Really, when one is that fat, one ought not to have soup!)

It was I whom Mother had singled out to do penance for Father's meanness. She would insist that I go over to Uncle's room: "You have to be nice to your poor uncle." Being "nice" entailed straddling his neck at his direction, with my legs firmly placed over his shoulders, and sliding down his back. This massage technique, he averred, did him a world of good. My reward was five groschen, with which I bought the latest serialized Austrian cartoon editions of Tom Sawyer, Robinson Crusoe, or Robin Hood.

Later on, when I was in boarding school in Alexandria, Uncle earned my mother's undying gratitude by coming once every few weeks to visit me and take me out. It was a special treat because my parents lived abroad at the time (after resigning from the diplomatic service, my father had taken up a post as an international arbitrator in Geneva) and so I rarely had visitors. But there was a price to be paid.

The outing went as follows: first we would stop at a little pastry shop called Flückiger, the best in Alexandria, run by a Swiss-Jewish couple who later emigrated to Europe and set up a bakery in Geneva. There my uncle would buy me a *coclo*, a vanilla ice cream cone with a hard chocolate glazing. Then he would go to a kiosk to purchase a newspaper. As he was terribly myopic, we would sit in one of the front rows in the cinema. He would spread his newspaper over his knees, and while I watched the current Tarzan movie or Gary Cooper Western and licked my *coclo*, he would place my free hand under the newspaper. I would fondle him there until I felt a mushy, sticky substance on my hand, not dissimilar to the ice cream, which would inevitably begin to run down the cone and ooze all over my other palm. After that, Uncle would close his eyes behind his thick, smoked glasses and would go to sleep until one of the irate neighbors nudged him from his snores.

When I grew older, a movie was no longer sufficient remuneration, so Uncle would give me a twenty-pound note. Such a windfall was extremely gratifying to me, because I was always without resources for treats. My parents had an aristocratic notion about how money spoils children: they must learn to be deserving. So our pocket money was meager; we were given only "useful" presents on our birthdays—no toys—and our clothes were mended and darned.

At fourteen, I was ashamed of my clothes. I went to a school for rich girls who loaded up on the latest Dior and Yves Saint Laurent fashions during their summer vacations, while I was wearing flounced dresses with Peter Pan collars, and pleated tartan skirts. On those rare occasions when I got to wear something more grown-up, it was usually some hand-me-down suit of my sister's, a relic of the late fifties that made me look frumpish and ungainly. It was clear to me that no Victoria College boy would look at me in those old-fashioned, shapeless clothes, which fitted me like a sack.

More than once I'd cried and begged Mother not to make me wear those dreadful clothes, but she wouldn't listen, she wouldn't see that she was ruining my prospects of getting a boyfriend. She remained entrenched in her belief that clothes ought to be worn until they're worn out, passed down from the older to the younger generation of children. If she bought us any clothes in Europe, it was usually one of those sturdy English tweed suits, from Harrods, which had every chance of outliving us all. In this way, after my sister had outgrown it and I had done my duty by it for the obligatory number of years, Mother still had a chance of inheriting it. If we protested against this recycling of clothes—for one thing, we were ashamed in front of our peers when Mother put in an appearance in the school lobby sporting her habitual grayish-green gabardine coat and her sensible English walking shoes—she would call us silly-billies, and take the occasion to launch into one of her interminable, edifying homilies about her aristocratic European friends, Baron So-and-so or Countess Such-and-such, who made it a point of dressing plainly, even shabbily, because they frowned on a display of wealth. One could tell the true aristocracy by the simplicity of their dress, she admonished.

When I gave her the example of my friends she scoffed: a bunch of Saudis and Kuwaitis with money and no class. Only a generation ago they were illiterate Bedouins on camelback; now they presumed to send their children to the English Girls College! The school oughtn't to admit so many Arabs. They were a bad influence on the other children.

I could see that any further effort at persuasion was wasted; my only chance to be stylish was Uncle's money.

One day, when I was thirteen, Uncle came to visit me at school. He kissed me chastely on the brow as I met him in the vestibule and slipped me an envelope with one hundred pounds—an astronomical sum for a child in those days. Then, without any further preamble, he led me to the Cecil, Alexandria's most luxurious grand hotel, where he had booked a room with a magnificent view of the sea. There he reminded me how fond he was of my parents and said that I should trust him: he would do nothing to dishonor my family; when he was done with me I would still be intact. I submitted to Uncle's instructions: I was to bare my rear and kneel on the bed, leaning forward on my elbows. The sensation was extremely painful at first and then not altogether disagreeable.

Years later, in trying to sort out for myself what it was that kept drawing me to those secret meetings at the Cecil Hotel, it was simple to say it was the money. Too simple. To be sure, my weakness was his money. I was greedy for it. But beyond that, I think I liked to exercise my power over him, to watch this flabby, sweaty, wheezing, loathsome creature plead for my favors, which I sometimes granted but which I just as often—quite unpredictably—withheld.

The pleasure of standing him up after a meeting had been arranged and paid for, of picturing him groaning with impatience in some sordid hotel room for that body which I was about to deny him, was at least as important to me as the money itself. And I found ample vindication for the indignities I was being subjected to at the hands of this man so esteemed by my family (who once beat his own daughter with clogs for refusing to marry, sight unseen, a suitor he had chosen for her) in being able to exact ever more exorbitant sums from him under the threat of blackmail.

In time I came to realize that Alex and I were just a pair of very fallible individuals united more by our weaknesses than by any pretense at consistency or fidelity.

There was nothing to forgive, nothing to explain. It was no longer essential to my happiness to be certain that I had supplanted everyone else in his life. The thought that Alex had men friends, even sold himself to them on occasion, had ceased to torment me. I had acquired a kind of indulgent tolerance toward him; after all, he compromised that part of me to which I attached the least importance: my reputation.

6

LOVE

FOR THE MOST PART, I had stopped thinking of love as a matter of affinity of character or correspondence of minds. I scrutinized my love for Alex even as I gave myself up to it, and I often wondered how I could care for a person about whom I found so much that was objectionable. I not only knew him to be grotesquely ignorant, with a conceit to match his ignorance. I had reason to believe him petty, vindictive—even cruel on occasion—and a liar. None of his answers to my questions about why he had changed jobs so often tallied with what I later learned from his former employers.

Alex claimed to have been very content with the job he held before coming to work for us, up until the day the owner's wife, an interfering bitch, decided to lend a hand in the liquor store. He had quit on account of this *puttana* (an Italian word for a whore, borrowed by the Greeks), he told me. The truth was that he had been fired. He had intrigued to get rid of the wife, whose presence in the store irked him because *he* wanted to be the boss, by convincing her that her husband had a mistress and was planning to convert secretly to Islam in order to take her as a second wife—a sheer fabrication, according to the owner, but his wife refused to believe him and walked out on him.

Another Greek, by the name of Bella, a flabby woman with very white skin and eyes brilliantly made up with kohl, whom I chanced to meet at the hairdresser's, confided to me that for years Alex had come to her house to give her a massage for a small fee. His massages were wonderful, but, she hastened to assure me, though he massaged her naked body, there had never been anything between them. He was like a "sister" to her, she added with a shrill laugh that seemed to tremble on the edge of madness. In no time at all, she became totally dependent on him: she would confide her secrets to him, seek counsel for her problems, and when she came home tired and disheartened, he would prepare for her a light meal and a lovely bath of warm milk, scented with vanilla beans, which he vouched did wonders for the skin.

For Alex, Bella's attraction must have lain precisely in her quintessential femininity: he could experience vicariously through her that which had been denied him. For it was impossible to escape the hold of this woman: her sultry scent, the languor of her movements, the bewitchment of her husky voice and hoarse laughter. She was a woman like none I had ever met: when she was not at the hairdresser's or engaged in lubricious gossip with a friend at the Café A l'Américaine, she seemed to pass the day trying out new facial powders, painting her eyelids with antimony, perfuming herself, freshening her breath with licorice juice—in short, preparing for love. (Her husband, a cabaret manager, I had never met, though I suspected he was an unsavory character; she had let slip that since he returned late at night and he did not want her to get bored waiting up for him, he allowed her to have "a friend" over from time to time in the evenings.)

The first time I had gone to see Bella, she had walked about the house barefoot, snake amulets around her ankles. I was mesmerized by the jingle of those amulets, the heat of her tread. She swished past me in a pink satin negligee with a very low neck, and seating herself unselfconsciously on her Oriental pouf, she went on painting her toenails, an act that exposed her plump legs to mid-thigh. She did not speak to me once while she was thus engaged: she needed all her concentration. Only the tip of her tongue moved feverishly over her rubied lips as she played with her ivory cigarette holder. But when she was done, she got up and prepared coffee for me, bringing it carefully to the boil three times in a tiny copper pot and serving it spiced with crushed cardamom seeds. Then, as I was drinking it, she narrated to me, between large mouthfuls of an overripe mango—its yellow juice trickling down her quivering, creamy breasts—that her friendship with Alex lasted until she made a new friend, Katerina. Alex, she said, was not in the least jealous of her men friends—on the contrary, he gave her useful tips on how to get and hold men—but he felt threatened by women. He was very hostile, in particular, to Katerina, who he felt was supplanting him in Bella's affections. Once when he was doing some ironing for her, he got into an argument with Katerina and threatened to hit her with the hot iron. Bella asked him never to set foot in her house again.

If this story did not appear fantastic to me, it is because I knew Alex's talent for anger—black, murderous fits of anger. I heard his screams one day, loud, fierce, lewd screams, and when I rushed to the kitchen I found Alex rolling on the ground with the cook—a woman of by no means negligible proportions. He was hitting and biting, pulling the hair of this *labwa* (Arabic for lioness; a word used pejoratively to denote a sexually voracious woman), refusing to let go, despite my intervention, until he had torn out a fistful. Alex may have owed his adventurous French to the European quarter he grew up in, with its babble of tongues, but his idiomatic Arabic he must have picked up in the street. His conversations—and quarrels—with our servants were punctuated by certain highly flavored words the likes of which had never been uttered in our house before.

If he did not dare vent his anger at my family in quite the same fashion, he nonetheless thought up subtly cruel ways of getting even for real or imagined wrongs. It came to my attention one morning when Alex was shaving my father that, playing on Father's vanity, he had succeeded in persuading him to submit to a painful ordeal by telling him that he had a forest of ugly black hairs growing inside his ears. Peering into the magnifying shaving mirror, Alex managed to portray to Father, who was feeble-sighted, the tiny tips of hairs he had plucked only days before as thick clumps clogging his ears. He searched them out one by one, down to the last solitary hair, grasping them between the prongs of his tweezers, with a look of ferocious concentration—the way a beast that had just sighted its prey might pause before pouncing and seizing the victim's hairy head between its fangs. When he had pulled out the last offensive hair with a theatrical jerk, stopping briefly to examine the disgusting specimen distastefully before discarding it, he then proceeded to spray out the wax from the ear canal with freezing water, despite Father's protestations, before scrubbing the inner folds with little balls of cotton soaked in alcohol, which he held with the dreaded tweezers. Thus had Alex been able to avenge himself on the old man.

For there were times Father could be quite overbearing, even though he seemed, on the whole, to have had a soft spot for Alex from the day he came to work with his melancholy air and his thirty or so useless years behind him. Alex resented being spoken to curtly, as though he were a servant—resented it all the more because he could not fall back on his white skin to compensate him for his social inferiority, Father himself being fair and blue-eyed. I had a feeling that Alex could not bear this natural distinction of Father's, any more than he could bear his dignified bearing, his personal charm, his facility with languages—he spoke Arabic, Turkish, French, English, German, and Italian flawlessly—his indomitable eloquence and self-assurance, which made his most frivolous statements seem important.

Even I was not sure I could place my trust in Alex's affection. I suspected that need had created in him an all-consuming egotism that made him incapable of the minimal loyalty that is the basis for a friendship: it sometimes appeared to me that though I would have done anything for him, he would not have lifted his little finger to help me. But I saw the emptiness in which he lived out his particular sorrow, and though I knew him to be selfish and untrue, I was totally imbued with him. I went after him, anticipating his every fall, ready to help him get back on his feet, to show him that his failure did not matter. If he needed my strength, garnered from reflection and introspection, I needed his weakness, because there I felt of use to him.

Perhaps empathy was my way of appropriating true experience, true suffering. I found myself almost seeking out his sorrow, a thing infinitely desirable in itself to someone like me, who had grown up in a harem-like cocoon, swaddled, almost anesthetized, from birth against any injurious contact with the outside world.

Beyond that, what was my real affinity for Alex? I think I understood the difficulty he had in trusting others, which was at the root of his fickleness. For though I had not been orphaned in my adolescence, I had known the dread of sudden abandonment, as the child of a diplomat. I had been shunted enough from boarding school to boarding school, from nanny to nanny, from foreign country to foreign country, to develop some of the same skepticism about lasting human bonds. I was not a hardened street kid like him; nor had I had to fend for myself since the age of sixteen. But I, too, had had to steel myself against the disappointments of parental love, during my childhood.

As for the attraction Alex felt for me, I do not believe it lay in anything I owned or anything I had achieved. I think what fascinated him about me was my dogged self-assertion, which, having nothing aggressive about it, did not threaten him. He sensed that despite its outward appearance of haphazardness and disorderliness, my course was firmly charted, and he had come to admire my way of life—its spontaneity, simplicity, and self-containment. He knew also that I was inner-oriented and could not be broken by others: my perfect indifference to public opinion intrigued him. It was this that he found so compelling, so utterly reassuring. Because it meant that no matter how ill one spoke of Alex, the value I placed on him was indestructible.

7

SHAME

EVERY SUNDAY *cette putain* goes to have her body laid bare by a filthy Greek. One of the "ladies" spotted them from her veranda, walking arm in arm. These verandas have no secrets from one another: all of Cairo—well-to-do Cairo—flocks to them in the summer to escape the heat. Late into the night you can hear the swish of palm trees brushing against their windowpanes, the syncopated rhythms of the Arab finger drum floating in from the ghostly feluccas on the Nile, the tinkling of the ice in the long, tall glasses filled with *karkade* (hibiscus tea), the murmur of platitudes, and the patter of *soufragis'* feet, gliding softly over the parquet floor to bring the homemade *salaisons*. (It was still considered a status symbol in Egypt to have an old black butler or cook well schooled by his former British masters.) This is how the Cairene "ladies" while away their summer months.

She is definitely no lady. The slut—she ought to be whipped, branded, put away for life. They say she's a pasha's daughter. Her poor parents know nothing about it, but it's only a matter of time. Her unmasking and disgrace are inevitable: news travels fast in Cairo. She is doomed. Already children have started pointing at her in the street, whispering. One day they'll be told by their mothers not to speak to the daughter of the Pasha anymore. She'll be isolated, quarantined, consigned to the infamy of pleasure.

I had a feeling my mother suspected something; she was watching me. Father surely knew, too. I observed his solitary fury; he was fighting now, not only against Time but against the equally intractable advance of changed times, when a daughter could go about with impunity because a father's word was no longer law—not even in the Orient. But my parents never talked to each other about this knowledge which they shared, the knowledge that their daughter was a whore.

One night I overheard Mother say to my sister that *la petite* was up to something; she could tell, she knew her daughter well. It was not normal for me to be so grave, so quiet—I, who was by nature so voluble. (It is true I had stopped talking to them: I was afraid of giving myself away by letting a word too many slip out. I spent most of my time locked up with a book in the impregnable solitude of my bedroom, contemplating from behind the barrier of my Harvard sophistication the uproar caused by Alex. Every breakfast, I sat at the table still wrapped in my voluptuous dreams and presented to my parents the same drowsy, shuttered face, the same bland voice from which nothing could be guessed of the secret, unimaginable delights of the previous afternoon. It was the thought of those delights which sustained me throughout the weary recurrent trivia of my daily life.)

My sister snickered. She told Mother not to worry: Alex wasn't really a man. But Mother was unrelenting: her daughter was in grave danger; she knew it—the danger of never being able to remarry, of not finding her place in Egyptian society. Pretty soon my sister began to see it her way. Like the rest of the family, she stopped speaking to Alex. If he tried to break the silence by making some casual remark or other, she acted as if she hadn't heard. No one could bear the sight of him anymore: he was an outrage, a "thorn" planted in their hearts, a reminder of their pain, their shame. Even I had stopped speaking to him in front of them, unless it was to transmit to him an order regarding something he should or should not do for Father. In their presence he ceased to be my lover, I acted as though he did not exist: I was ashamed of him.

Soon this silent war of nerves became unendurable. A family council was called to discuss the Alex affair. Panic-stricken at the thought that they would kick Alex out, that I'd never see him again, I pleaded his case far better than that indolent fatalist would have deigned to do for himself had he been allowed to attend the meeting. I stressed his devotion to Father, his willingness to work double shifts, the difficulty of finding a suitable replacement, given the absence of private nursing agencies in Egypt. But these arguments carried no weight with my sister, who, far from being alarmed at the prospect of losing Alex, would surely have been glad to have seen him dismissed in order to have an excuse to take his place. She would have stood behind Father's rattan chair and waited on him hand and foot: she would not have minded—perhaps would even have welcomed—the chance to lead him to the toilet, the way Alex did, and would have wiped his behind proudly, tenderly, even gloatingly. As for Mother, she remained entrenched in her belief that Alex was *une vraie ordure* (real scum), that under his display of selfless devotion for Father lay the most aberrant cunning, that with ruthless deliberation he had marked me as a prospective bride, whose family name and dowry would help him achieve the respectability he so desperately sought. What better way for *quelqu'un de bas étage*, someone from the gutter, as she put it—and someone with a disreputable past to boot—to force himself down the throat of censorious public opinion than to acquire a stainless, unimpeachable man like my father for a father-in-law.

It was left to Father, as head of the family, to decide how this "shameless adventurer" should be dealt with. Much to the surprise of everyone—especially Mother, who was dismayed to see how relatively little my "virtue" weighed for him against the scale of his imperative need for Alex—he decided at first against firing him, saying he would have a serious talk with him instead. I wondered whether Father's unexpected resolution was not subconsciously the gesture of a lonely man toward the only wholehearted admirer left to him: he needed an audience.

Alex, I had always suspected, felt rather drawn to Father's solitary figure in his high-backed rattan chair, with his tired, watery blue eyes and his world-weary voice and manner. He enjoyed making Father the herbal teas that he took three times a day, after every meal, to ensure a good digestion, and listening to his interminable monologues about a life which, having long ago lost its vital momentum, flickered on in the labyrinths of his memory. More than once I thought I detected in Alex's appraising eyes a sort of compassionate curiosity for Father, mixed with admiration. And Father was certainly not unwilling to accept the burden of that guileless admiration. Even if he himself was only able to reciprocate with the condescension bred of his class, he was nonetheless happy to spread out the riches of his culture and breeding—and even of his clothing—before Alex's appreciative eyes. For while his ancient suits were no longer as well pressed and brushed as they had once been, they were, as Father himself liked to point out, woven of the finest English wools, and their cut imparted to his lean, aristocratic figure a certain determined elegance.

One day Father called Alex and asked him, "Perhaps you imagine, young man, that by insinuating yourself into our company you'll be able to use our daughter as a springboard for your personal ambitions?" To this unanswerable, staggering injustice Alex proffered no reply, beyond saying that they should not argue about him—of all the thankless subjects. Father then went on to tell him that if he hoped to make his fortune by marrying me he should reckon on my being disinherited, thrown out of the house, banned from the family circle.

When this threat failed to bring about the desired result, Mother addressed herself to me; repeating her favorite sermon for the *n*th time, in that afflicted tone of voice which was peculiarly her own, about how my father might not be leaving me a great fortune, because he did not steal and accept bribes in public office like so many of his colleagues, but was leaving me one thing money could not buy: a reputation of gold. His integrity had brought him the respect of old and new regime alike. I was not to bring him dishonor in his old age!

I reacted to Mother's indignation over my relationship with Alex as to a fetish-ridden moral hang-up not deserving of a reply, much the way I had in adolescence to her outrage over the loss of my virginity. Before my sarcastic response, Mother let out a cry of rage, she beat me, screamed for everyone to hear that her daughter was a *sharmouta* (dirty rag; a term used to refer to a prostitute in Egypt), a *kalba*, a bitch. Then she began to weep for herself—to ask Allah what she had done to deserve such a fate—and for her poor disgraced child who was not fit to live in the Orient. Didn't I know that a woman was lost here without her reputation? No one would marry me now.

"What else are you going to do to your father? There's nothing left but for you to go down into the street and open your legs!" she exclaimed, her hands writhing pitiably.

I was moved in spite of myself by her hysterical weeping. I tried to reassure her, to tell her there was nothing between Alex and me: how could she think I'd stoop to have an affair with a *pédé*, a fairy! But Mother silenced me with a regally tragic gesture. And when I tried to take her in my arms, she pushed me back and rushed out of the room. I could hear her yell, as she locked the door, that she'd never let me out, she'd rather see me die of hunger than live to have my body fondled by that *ordure*.

I felt the same kind of humiliation I had felt when I had fallen from a horse on my cousin's farm at the age of nine and bled. Mother had forced me to undress before the doctor whom she had brought to make sure I was still intact. I had not forgotten the feel of those cold, slithering fingers invading my privates or the pain at the prodding—as though he were pinching me very hard—or my sister's venomous smile when I came out of my room after the "examination" was over, my cheeks crimson with shame and rage.

For my sister and I had never got along; our characters, dispositions, tastes could not be more different. It was always clear to me that she hated me, felt I was in the way, that my birth dethroned her in Father's affection (my sister adored Father). Not a day went by without a fight, a violent, bloody fight, even though Mother claimed she had brought me into this world so my sister could have a playmate and even though she wailed that a sister was one's best friend, that it was so sad we didn't get along, and what would happen to us after she'd gone?

In the end, my parents decided to fire Alex. Once they had made up their minds, they remained adamant, despite my tearful entreaties and my threats to follow him.

At first Alex turned down my offer to join him, claiming that I would not be able to stand the contact with so much that was common and ugly on Antiquity Street. But I retorted that he just didn't have the guts to love me in opposition to my family, to possess me and take me away: I was more than prepared to resign myself to the seediness of his apartment and to give up the niceties of the toilet for his sake, I said.

And indeed, in the weeks that followed my departure from the house, I was in a state of exhilaration as I strolled about his neighborhood, visiting with him all manner of vulgar establishments, from disreputable Greek tavernas to shady bars, poking my head into the windows of third-rate jewelers, selecting all kinds of abominable objects for our house—the kind of knick-knacks that found favor on Antiquity Street. I derived extreme satisfaction from the thought that, like him, I now belonged to that aggrieved body commonly referred to as the lower class.

Alex maintained that I would not be able to keep up this existence for long, that once the novelty had worn off I would run back to the comforts of Zamalik. I was at pains to prove him wrong; I made a point of dressing as shabbily as possible, always selecting clothes which looked as though they had been knocked about in a great deal, making sure that there was a note of disrepair in my apparel—a hole in my jeans, a stain on my shirt. Alex laughed with scorn at these efforts, saying I remained unmistakably upper-class in my shabby clothing—and in my overdone attempts to find everyone and everything charming and curious.

Yet I was genuinely enchanted with my life on Antiquity Street; it appealed to my love for out-of-the-way nooks. My restless feet continued to tread the narrow, crooked lanes in search of adventure. My taste for exploration found expression both in my new domesticity—in trying, with my reduced means, to conjure a little beauty in the blighted space we shared—and in the strange encounters I had under Alex's auspices. I entertained romantic fantasies about all sorts of dubious types, deriving extreme diversion from their outrageous stories, following them with my imagination—and sometimes with my footsteps—through all kinds of vivid episodes. I felt I was an extraordinarily privileged mortal to have run into them.

Antiquity Street had become home to me, not just a place I occasionally had to drive through, a handkerchief held to my nose, on my way back across the Abou 'Ela Bridge to the civilized part of town. I had ceased to notice the smell that was so repellent to me on the first day—a smell, was it of decomposing garbage? of sewers? of rat pellets dropped behind staircases? It had acquired a familiarity that made me no longer mind it. In fact, later, when I was in a less malodorous place, I remembered it nostalgically and would gladly have substituted it for the clean, pungent scent of the New England pines that my Cambridge bedroom windows overlooked.

Alas! The delights of slumming were cut short one morning by the arrival of the chauffeur my parents had sent to invite us both back. Of the two afflictions, it seemed they preferred putting up with Alex to the disgrace of our living together.

8

DEVOTION

WHEN I WAS LITTLE I had murderous fits of rage. I resented Mother's complete, self-effacing devotion to Father: I could not bear to see her standing there like a shadow at the doorway, as though she had no right to take up any of Father's space, watching anxiously for the slightest hint of his displeasure at her having forgotten to bring him something (God forbid! the salt!) or done something wrong (not removing his soft-boiled egg in time from the boiling water) or failed to do something (replenishing his glass of orange juice), by oversight. I wanted to get back at that object of utter, abnegating devotion by depriving him of the only thing he cared for in life: his reputation for probity among his fellow men. Better still, I wanted to kill him to save my mother from being so used, so abused. I wanted him to die so she would have a few years left to live just for herself for a change. My mother did not understand what was becoming of me as a result of witnessing her unhappiness. But even if she had, how could she have concealed from me what was so plainly written on her face? It was from her face, not from Simone de Beauvoir's *Second Sex*, which I perused at the age of twelve with the slightly blasé air of a child who had already learned this lesson, that I drew the resolve to save myself from the domestic tyranny which poor Mother accepted uncomplainingly as all that a woman could hope for from life.

I never shared my thoughts with anyone. I was afraid of them, afraid of myself, afraid of God. Instead, every night, before going to bed, I prayed fervently for the prolongation of Father's life. But I think my secret wish to see him die was also a way of punishing Mother by depriving her of that husband of hers whom she loved so much, so badly—whom she loved at my expense. Had she not sent me off to boarding school at the age of five in order to have more time to devote to his service? Had she not left me during my school vacations in the hands of nannies so that she could go off with him to his favorite spas? "Go away, you awful woman, I want my mother," I had reportedly told Miss Duffy, in whose care I had been left when I was seven, while Mother was off skiing with Father in Chamonix. Miss Duffy had gone. And after her, in rapid succession, Miss Boden, Miss Scanlon, Fräulein Winterhof—all of them had resigned on account of my "deplorable conduct." But while I had succeeded in driving them away, I had not succeeded in winning Mother back. She did not have the energy for me. So off I went again to boarding school. "*Il lui fallait une mère beaucoup plus jeune*"—she should have had a much younger mother—she often told her friends of her *enfant difficile*. Five nannies, eight boarding schools by the age of eleven . . . always expelled for insubordination.

Mother spied on me throughout my adolescence, opening my mail, listening in on my telephone conversations, even checking my handbag for condoms and my underwear for stains while I was in the bathtub. Unlike Father, Mother was not able to breach the barrier of Egyptian habit; her roots were deep in the village where her father had owned land; she never succeeded in freeing herself from the net of parental authority. I hated her for the sordid, obsessive way she would repeat to me, "*J'espère que tu vas te marier en blanc*": I hope you will marry in white.

My mother, my love. Sadly, she could not extend her affection to me outside of her own ingrown little world, which stifled me and often revolted me.

By contrast, I loved Father for his broad-mindedness and his tact in these matters as in all others, a remarkable thing when one considers that he was born at the end of the nineteenth century and that his childhood was spent in a harem entourage. It was he who, despite his fondness for my husband, had stood by me in the stressful days of the divorce. (When Mother complained that I had about as much regard for my husband's name as I had for the respectable labels in my dresses, Father had told her it should come as no surprise that my sharp, ironic mind and audacious personality had not been able to tolerate for long the simple dullness of my husband's company.)

I used to swell with pride as a little girl when people told me, "*Inti tala le abouki*" (you take after your father), which I took to mean that my qualities were but a smaller, more wayward version of his. My rebelliousness was to his independence of mind what my stubborn pride was to his integrity: lips sealed, despite the blows that rained on me—never say sorry if you are in the right.

Father's pride and integrity made an imprint on me at a very tender age, in the course of a chance encounter with King Farouk in the lobby of the Hôtel du Rhône, where we used to stay in Geneva. The King, who had recently been deposed, had stalked past us in the direction of the reception desk, when Father followed him, saying, "Don't you recognize me anymore?"

"Of course I recognize you, Pasha!" the King answered. "But I was not sure you would want to shake hands with me in public. All the Egyptians who used to kiss my hands pretend now they don't see me."

To which my father replied, "But, Majesty, *I* never kissed your hands, therefore I am not afraid to greet you in public."

It was this father, so loved and hated, who was my model throughout my growing years—not my mother. I spent hours observing his every gesture in company: the graceful, dignified way in which he moved from guest to guest, uttering labored politenesses. How happy I was when Father, noticing me at last, would hold out his arms to me before the sleek, distinguished-looking gentlemen with the gray temples and their elegantly clad wives who were assembled for tea. I would run up to him and nestle contentedly in his lap, from which I had a view of the Nile out of the salon's big bay window with the Nile-colored satin drapes. Dreamily, I would observe the palm trees bordering the river, their windswept branches moving slowly, in circular motions. The male palms, tall, sleek, with luminous white trunks, seemed to me so much handsomer than the female ones. The latter, short, squat, stunted, and dumpy, swayed heavily beneath the burden of the red dates at their crests.

Father would stroke my hair, and his tone would be playful and tender when he spoke about me to his guests. He was proud of his daughter. I, too, was proud of him: I admired his wit, charm, and erudition. Trusting and blind as a newborn babe in his arms, I could not yet perceive that behind the stylized gallantry of his perfect Henri Quatre breeding, he was as aggressive and selfish as any home-raised Egyptian male.

9

ISOLATION

ONE WEEKEND, Alex failed to return at the end of his day off. For three days, he gave no sign of life, and I was ill with fear that he had grown tired of me and would never come back. After all, what did I have to give him that he could not get elsewhere? What could someone like him, who had exhausted pleasures, want with my amateurish lovemaking and bookish talk?

At last, when I could bear it no longer, I went over to his apartment in search of him. The sun was so ferocious that the palms lining the Nile were burned to the color of coffee. Sluggishly, that great river was making its way toward the Mediterranean, where it would empty; its waters flowing slowly, silently away from its banks like blood flowing out of a body, leaving them exposed. Some of that same sluggishness had even overtaken the children who normally bathed in it, the children of the poor. For now, no barefoot children were to be seen along its desiccated banks, no graceful feluccas with flocks of birds hovering over their lean hulls, outstretched wings flashing and gleaming in the sunlight. It was the low season.

The day was heating up, and down on Antiquity Street a few old Greeks sat out on their front porches fanning themselves listlessly with their newspapers and munching fly-blackened bananas. They remained like this, silent for hours on end, because, having lived so long in close proximity, they already knew everything there was to know about one another; there was little left to gossip about. But occasionally, when a stranger strayed into their neighborhood, one of them would rouse himself from his torpor in order to pipe out that precious piece of news; it would be passed along from porch to porch. If the intruder happened to be a man, he might even be greeted with a "*Yassou re malaka!*" (literally, "Hello there, masturbator") and hear a cackle behind him.

I could see them wagging their heads and sucking

their toothless gums as I passed, and I had the distinct feeling they were trying to say something to me, a greeting, perhaps, after their fashion. It was not meant to be unfriendly, yet, I don't know why, it made me uncomfortable to see these old men eyeing me and angling their heads from side to side.

Farther down, two inveterate Greeks, thin as rakes, stood stooped over their canes exchanging *kalimeras* (good mornings) in tremulous voices. The street cats nearby howled as they mated. One of the men hissed at them, striking the ground with his cane, and the cats scattered. I cast a smile in his direction, for I recognized this fellow: I had been up and down Antiquity Street scores of times. But there was not a single glint of recognition in his eyes, nothing—only a dull glow in a nest of wrinkles. It was this that struck me most about their faces; one could not see their eyes. It struck me with a sort of horror because I could not help thinking that these individuals had perhaps once been the luminaries of a great civilization.

A handful of shriveled women with haggard, lifeless faces huddled at the entrance of Alex's building. They were dressed in that eternal black which Greek women in the Orient seem to wear all of their life, whether for dead father, husband, or son—no one knows—and they were plucking the unfortunate chicken that had been chosen for that day's meal; the stairs were plastered with blood and feathers. Their paunches hung over their knees, and the jutting veins in their hands told of many hours of cooking and washing for their children who had since grown up and left for Athens, Sydney, and New York.

As I tried to thread my way between the mounds of doomed poultry piled up on the stairs—which appeared not to have been swept since the day the mason laid down his tools—the women gazed past me with expressionless faces, as though they had made a silent collective decision to have nothing to do with my affair with Alex. But from the rustling of whispers behind my back, from the words *ofoukaras* (poor thing), *kolopetho* (fairy) that reached my ears as I continued my climb, I had the odd feeling that these immobile women were conspiring with the heat and the dust to bring Alex down. Yet somehow I looked upon these old harpies with indulgence: they were so withered, so clearly of the people.

I let myself into Alex's dim little apartment. The half-light was familiar to me, for Alex was in the habit of closing all the shutters during the day, reopening them only in the evenings when the burning air had dissipated and had been replaced by the night breezes. What a delight it had always been to lie down in that cool bedroom, saturated with incense, at siesta time, with nothing to disturb those languid hours but the overhead flutter of geese and the clucking of chickens that were being raised on the roof.

At six, we would get up and go outside to the breezy balcony, overlooking the citrus grove. We would watch the evening light filter through the essence of oranges, as we munched our watermelon slivers and inhaled the heady scent of jasmine, which wafted up to us from the garden below.

We would sit together like this until the wee hours of the morning, interspersing our conversations and laughter with long pauses, during which we simply looked at each other with sympathetic eyes, the way two very old friends who feel comfortable with each other might. There was something soothing about the cadence of those silences. There was a restful domestic quietude, too, in the way we sat and listened to Alex's creaky old phonograph, in the way he played with his cat on the ledge with the poinsettias in bloom, in his light, airy footsteps, in the graceful way he folded and unfolded the old straw mat on which we sometimes lay when it was too hot to sleep inside. (On especially humid afternoons, we felt as if drugged; the giant fan in the middle of the bedroom ceiling, a rusty grating fan that lulled us to sleep, would stop working every so often and we would wake up, suffocating, from our siesta and seek refuge under the sun-bleached canopy on the balcony.)

I walk over to him, very quietly, sitting down next to him on the bed without a word. For a long time he just lies there, listless and taciturn, staring out of his spade-shaped window with the fluttering gauze curtain. I wait, holding his hand in mine as I look at the fair curls circling his ears, the down on the slender nape of his neck, which the sun faintly touches with gold, the slow intake and release of the flowery curtain.

It's past midnight now. We talk in whispers, Alex and I, our faces pressed close together. Alex says he understands my mother, this dishonor, having to face the frightful contempt of the Cairo drawing rooms, being aware that each and every one of the friends who come to see her in the salon—hung with the large Gobelin wall tapestry displaying a shepherdess and her lover fondling under a willow tree—*knows* even if they do not say a word about it, because what tactful words could they possibly find to soften the blow? No, Alex understands very well that she should have beaten me the way she did. If I were his daughter, he would have beaten me till I was black and blue. Suddenly I realize that Alex does not understand me; he has never understood me and he never will. He is unable to understand such perversity. It's no wonder: I myself find it hard, sometimes, to believe that I am able to cross my parents so calmly, with such determination.

Alex has noticed my pained expression. Casting a roguish look in my direction, he sticks out his tongue at me. He tells me not to look so shocked. He is a Greek, after all. Greek men, like all Mediterraneans, are terrible cads; they cheat on their wives like crazy, but if one so much as suspects his wife of being unfaithful, he'll beat her, disfigure her, maim her—even kill her. He laughs. With amazing suddenness, he has become his mischievous, irrepressible old self again. He slips out from his sheets and begins to execute a pas de deux, encircling me, twirling devilishly fast around me, performing pirouettes with ever-greater speed. I have to chase him back to bed.

We talk now about day-to-day events—not about the future. We know we cannot possibly have a life together.

Only in Sidi Kreir do we seem to have a refuge from the invasive, vulgar, gossiping, malevolent world of Cairo. Only there, in our desert home, once we have climbed to the top of the roof by way of the spiral staircase leading out of the inner courtyard, and have lain in each other's arms listening to the incomparable music of the fountain below and watching the magnificent spectacle above of the green-bellied, bee-eating migratory birds that arrive from Europe in huge waves in early September, do we sometimes nurse the illusion that here at last it is possible to work out a common future, slowly, in seclusion and in harmony with nature.

In Sidi Kreir, Alex's love brings me peace for all too short a while. It is strangely like the enchantment, the spell of the house itself, with its artesian well, its gaslit interior, and its windmills silhouetted against the sky, which pump water for the fig trees riding the sand dunes.

I would have liked to tell Mother about the glimpse I caught of Alex this morning, through the door that had come ajar.

He is naked under the shower, within arm's reach,

sublime. The goldenness of that back, of that small, hard bottom, is such as I've never seen, never touched. The body is perfect: nothing can compare to the harmony of its colors, to the balance between the slender limbs with the narrow hips and that chest, smooth as a bust of Donatello's. Nothing on earth can be more extraordinary than the way that body bears its member like some peerless treasure proffered to the hands. I want to touch it, to caress its inexpressible softness, to feel it in my mouth. I want to shut my eyes and find myself transported to the little flat across the bridge, where every Sunday, pleasures are imparted to me that make me cry out in rapture. But Alex surprises me peeking at him and drives me off, by sprinkling water into my eyes.

Alas! Mother would never have been able to understand the violence of my passion. She had never known pleasure. One day, when she was twelve, a black-veiled, one-eyed woman with a face as wizened as a raisin arrived at her father's estate from the village. Mother ran for her life when she saw her take out a long, thin shaving knife that looked like the ones she had seen used on the geese's necks. For it was considered a *sunna*, a good deed, in Islam to let the blood flow: her father had explained to her that unlike the Christians, who killed their animals by strangulation, the Muslims killed them in a far more humane manner, by severing the jugular vein. But Mother had not been convinced; she had fled from the scene of carnage, just as she did now, even though the two eunuchs, who were in hot pursuit, called out after her that the old woman had come to perform a *sunna*. Mother screamed so loud the mango trees shook at her passage. But it availed her nothing; the eunuchs caught up with her and dragged her back to the portico. One of them pinned her to the floor by sitting astride her belly, while the other one wrenched her legs open, so the midwife could sprinkle her slippery kernel with flour, to get a good grip on it.

For three days after that, Mother lay in a fever, her body in convulsion like a slaughtered lamb, her head in perpetual motion from right to left and left to right like someone trapped in a circle of dancing dervishes: she kept hearing the soft, toothless cackle of the old hag, with the expert fingers, long and thin like her father's brown cigarillos, as she sharpened her shaving knife against a flint stone. Even after the fever had abated, and the infection had been brought under control by a doctor called in from Cairo, who told her *dada* to discontinue the use of ground-up *sous al kutn*, the little insects that built their nests in the cotton plants when they were stored on the rooftops of the village houses, and to resort instead to alcohol as a disinfectant, Mother went on shuddering whenever her arm brushed against the amulet she had been forced to wear for a month, as a prevention against future sterility, should anyone have put the evil eye on her during her clitoridectomy. It consisted of a cloth, which had been pinned onto her collar, containing a shriveled, bluish-black, putrescent, grapelike piece of flesh: her own.

On the third day, Mother regained consciousness and her *dada*, who believed the devil had been exorcised out of her, thanks to his *helba* (a drink of fenugreek popularly believed to have a soothing effect on the nerves), praised the Merciful One. When Mother cried because the alcohol he was applying to her open wound felt like fire between her legs, he told her to resign herself to Allah's will; he himself had had to undergo a similar ordeal when he was only half her age. And then he recounted to her how he had been kidnapped from his family when he was seven years old and brought by camel caravan to Egypt, together with a group of children from neighboring African villages, who had been bound hand and foot and herded together like cattle in the back of a cart containing elephant tusks, saltpeter, coffee, ostrich plumes, and leopard skins. Of all these cargoes the slaves were the most valuable. Cowed by the exhaustion of many days and nights of travel across the desert, by hunger and thirst, and by the beatings that had rained on them throughout the trip, the children submitted meekly to having their testicles cut off on arrival in Egypt. They were then half-buried in the hot sand, which was believed to have antiseptic qualities, until their wounds dried up.

I slipped my hand under the sheet and caressed Alex: I could feel his ribs in the dark. He was thin, frail, vulnerable. It was precisely this weakness that transported me with pleasure: what a pleasant change from the Mediterranean virility of Egyptians, shirts open over hairy chests. There was no hair on Alex's chest, nothing masculine about him beyond his sex. Even that, small, soft, delicately pink, had about it a childish quality that brought to mind cherubs in a Botticelli painting.

Alex once said jokingly that it had something to do with growing up in too strong a sun. He blamed everything on the heat—his stunted member, his liver ailment, his crankiness, his financial failure. In another country, he would have been a millionaire. Even Greece, *ce pays misérable*, was now a better place to live in than Egypt. If only he could get away, emigrate. But he was stuck. He had no money; he couldn't even pay for a damn ticket. He alternated in this fashion between thinking the curse was on him and his family and thinking it was on the land itself where his ancestors had chosen to establish their line: yes, Egypt itself was primed for doom. He was sure of it.

I listened to him. He spoke with the same theatricality as he made love—a theatricality at once contrived and genuine. (Once when he asked me why I did not dress in a manner more befitting my station in life, the way my mother wished me to, I was on the verge of replying irritably that I did not care for fancy dresses: I wanted people to accept me for myself. But I held my tongue out of a kind of delicacy, thinking that that was precisely what Alex could not do: be his own character. He was destined to go through life as an actor, to conceal his self—if indeed he had a self—behind a mask. With a charmer's sincerity that even he believed in, he managed to manipulate men and women alike.)

And despite his braggadocio, I suspected he was prey to an old, familiar fear, the fear of being a stranger after all these years and of remaining one till his dying day —not that it made it any less hard for him to leave Egypt and settle elsewhere.

All of a sudden he pulled me toward him and, nestling his head in the crook of my left arm, told me, "*Balance-toi sur moi*"—Ride me.

For a long time I stayed like this, riveted, moaning above the din of the city. The noise that came up to the sweltering flat, stilled only at siesta, was unimaginable. Honking horns, screeching brakes, wailing radios, strident voices, ear-splitting guttural cries: no one merely talked in Egypt; people shouted. In the evening, people sat out on their balconies to escape their sun-baked apartments. They called out to one another the latest rumor about the neighbor across the hall, who had taken a second wife, about *Khawaga* Papadopoulos, who came home dead-drunk and beat his wife, about Maria Guarini, the new neighbor, who paraded in sluttish attire, the shameless woman, about Zeinab, who jinxed a rival by putting a drop of menstrual blood in her coffee, about Ahmad, who caught a rat and buried it live in front of his doorstep for good luck, by the Prophet!

Those people too poor to afford flats with balconies sat out on the stairs: they slaughtered their fowl on the stairs, picked over their rice on the stairs, had their palms read on the stairs, quarreled on the stairs, and made up on the stairs.

I listened to all this through the paper-thin walls, while Alex dozed. I watched the shadows of people going by on the blinds. When it seemed that there were crowds of them, hordes of them, all of them going through our room, I knew evening was approaching. People must be gathering their children together, going home. I, too, must leave.

I roused Alex from his sleep, told him I felt sad. (I was returning to the United States in two days' time—but I had not yet told Alex.) He said it was the heat affecting me, making me feel tired and depressed. And he suggested we go out for dinner.

He capered down the narrow staircase into the street, like a schoolboy, disturbing in the process half a dozen or so emaciated dogs, who were milling about the entrance. Then he took the last few steps in a single bound. I half expected him to break into a dance along Antiquity Street, the way he did at home, traversing our long corridor in a series of rapid, scissorlike écartés—but no. He stopped suddenly at the bottom of the staircase, pushed back his straw hat with his thumb—a gesture that I knew to be accompanied by the performance of a little smile—and addressed a three-legged dog amiably. "Yes, you and I have certainly known better times, my friend." The dog hobbled off, disappearing under the stairs. I followed Alex with a heavy heart, trying to imitate the easy saunter he affected.

We headed for the old city, where, in the smoking ant heap of the medieval town, among the many mosques with the graceful spires and colorful domes, among the little booths stacked with gaily painted earthenware pottery, with gleaming pots of brass and copper, with blue-stained blown glasses and vases, among the glittering precious stones and warm gold of antique shops, among the native cafés with flaring ovens, in which whole sheep could be seen turning on spits, among the narrow, winding lanes with the smells of charcoal-broiled corn, of roasted peanuts, of burnt sugar, of sandalwood incense and musk—lanes resonating with the clinking of coins in the beggars' old cans, the gurgle of nargilehs, the clanking tin cups of the buffalo-milk hawkers, the deafening clamors of *Roba bichia* (from the Italian *roba vecchia*, a cry harking back to the time when most of Egypt's vendors of secondhand clothes were Italians), the whining of branded camels on their way to the slaughterhouse, the hee-haws of bowlegged mules laden with clover, the heart-rending trill of canaries, whose eyes had been gouged out in the belief that if they could not see the world they would sing more sweetly—nestled a humble little restaurant whose specialty was *mulukhiyya*, a green soup made from an herb called Jew's mallow, which Alex and I loved.

While I sat slaking my thirst with pomegranate juice, I studied Alex with amusement: there was something incongruous about him, dressed in his fine pale gray silk suit and Dior ascot, eagerly tackling a fat pickled eggplant whose decomposing, purplish flesh and overripe seeds, bursting out of its guts, seemed to make his mouth water. All of a sudden he raised his eyes from his *mezze*, and for the second time that evening our eyes met in a long look of longing. Our hands linked under the table.

While we waited for our food we watched the canvas of Egyptian life unroll before us as Cairo awoke from its daily sun-drugged afternoon stupor: the paunchy, bead-twirling sheikh in a keffiyeh seated on a low stool in the café, slurping mint tea out of a small, gold-ringed glass; his camel resting nearby, solemnly chewing on his cud and exposing his gums in the process in a manner that rather reminded me of my toothless, eighty-year-old aunt who went on chewing sugar-cane sticks up to her dying day; the nargileh washer who stepped out onto the sidewalk to empty the slop from the water bowls, and then lined them up in colorful rows along the wall (each customer brought his own mouthpiece); the fat government clerk, whose paunch stuck out preposterously from under his stained lightweight brown suit, gnashing his chicken bones noisily, and picking the gristle from between his teeth with the long, manicured fingernail of his pinkie, while next to him a Coptic monk in a black habit, with dark, haunting eyes straight out of a Byzantine fresco, was dipping his long beard into his gravy; the scruffy little boys kneeling on the ground, playing *Siga*, a game in which pebbles are used as pieces and the board is composed of squares cut into the mud pavement; the scribe squatting on the curb who for a small fee will write dangerous love letters for illiterate village girls; the blind cantor with the smoky dark glasses, swaying to the rhythm of the hundred holy names; the butcher whose dripping gobbets of bloody meat, hooked up in front of the store, seemed to attract ogling crowds, in much the same way as the sugar dolls for the *mulid*, the Prophet's birthday, in the next-door confectionery, attracted swarms of ravenous flies, while out on the same dilapidated sidewalk, running down the row of close-set shabby shops, sat the butcher's neighbor, the leatherworker, skillfully transforming all manner of leftovers—cows' hooves, calf bellies, sheepskin

—into suitcases, handbags, and purses; the dustman sweeping up the road with his long brooms made of rushes, carefully gathering together into neat piles the watermelon rinds, corncobs, peanut shells, date pits, pomegranate peels, oily paper falafel cones, and guava juice cans; the street sprinkler, who caused the grateful passersby—barefoot men, donkeys, mules, camels, horses—to feel a delightful tingle in their limbs as the cold water splattered down the burning pavement, soothing their tired feet (he got a big baksheesh for spraying the drawn blinds of cabaret *Lu'lu'* [pearl] with cold water scented with rose petals, every hour on the hour, to cool and perfume it for the evening belly-dance performance); the garbage collector with the open, donkey-drawn cart of fly-blown refuse, driving his heavily laden animal with whip and with angry curses up the tortuous side alleys. (The beasts of burden in Egypt were invariably skin on bones, their owners being too poor to feed themselves, let alone their animals.)

As I watched the scene, old memories stirred. I saw that other donkey: a bony, underfed beast trying to lug a cart loaded with the huge Stillman piano that was being moved into my aunt's farmhouse, in the village of Ragalat. The donkey's owner goaded him on by accompanying the blows with a volley of abuse, and whenever the poor exhausted creature ground to a halt, he would jolt him forward by jabbing his bleeding flank—poking a stick right into the open, festering sore on his haunch. When I cringed at this sight, turning my face away, my aunt laughed at me, saying I would do better to pity the donkey's owner, whose life was hard and brutish, than to waste my tears on a donkey. (I never liked my aunt; she was like most of the elder women in the family: distinguished, cold, haughty, living at the mercy of their prejudices.)

My aunt had a beautiful country estate overlooking the Nile within a stone's throw of the foul-smelling mud hovels of her poor tenants, who huddled with their large families and animals in one wretched room. They had to go outside to the wasteland to answer the call of nature, and, on cold nights, they slept over their manure-fueled ovens with their numerous offspring strewn around them in a huddle, like a litter of piglets. On Friday, the Muslim day off, there would often be a family reunion at my aunt's. While the grownups picnicked out on the terrace, overlooking the riverbank with the tall papyrus stalks, gorging themselves on pigeons stuffed with rice and pine nuts and on *Eish el Seray*, "palace bread," a rich pastry soaked in syrup and covered with a buffalo cream so thick it could be cut with a knife, the children played in the magnificent garden where the air was heavy with the sweet, rich smell of mangoes and the trees rang with the call of partridges. They would skip along the edge of the narrow canals with the sound of gurgling water, which led to a pond rimmed with fig trees.

Of all the children present on these occasions, my favorite was my aunt's son. He and I always banded together, and we were the terror of the family. We would sneak into my aunt's bedroom and blacken our eyes, pirate style, with her eyebrow pencil, ignoring her injunction that we were not to touch her things, and then we would engage in rowdy, sometimes violent games of cops and robbers or cowboys and Indians, hurling ourselves onto her settee, delicately upholstered in pale silks, jumping off the dainty gilded arms of her brocaded Louis Quinze chairs—games that inevitably ended with some priceless object being damaged or broken and with us receiving a thrashing. Nothing could daunt our spirit, however, and I, being a girl, always felt honor-bound to outdo my cousin in the game of brinkmanship, which ranged from swinging on the branch of the highest tree, like Tarzan, to venturing down some dark, treacherous village road by night, in search of the "haunted" shed with the "voracious" bats, to tearing across the village on horseback, scattering the terrified chickens by our passage, to sliding down from our second-floor bedroom window on knotted sheets, like the prisoner of Zenda —bravery, in short, inspired by the latest American movie we had seen.

In those days, I prided myself on being a tomboy, and was at pains to prove that I had more pluck than my cousin, because I had just suffered a major setback at school, that of being spurned for the role of Othello on the grounds that I was too "feminine." This was insult added to injury, one that I bore with little grace despite the emphasis of my English education on being a "good sport," because I was accustomed to getting the main part and had just had my ego inflated by rave reviews in the *Journal d'Egypte* for my performance of Eliza Doolittle. With the memory of this slight still rankling, I accepted all of my cousin's dares, all, that is, except one: that of swallowing live locusts. To impress me, my cousin would catch the locusts and, snapping off their heads and feet, crunch a handful with glee—a trick he learned from a Kuwaiti friend in Victoria College, who told him these were considered a great delicacy in his country. I watched my cousin's repertoire even though it made my stomach wrench, in order not to be considered a "bloody bore"—his favorite epithet for other members of the family. What I simply could not bring myself to do was to witness the scene of carnage that took place every year during Id el Adha, after the pilgrimage to the Kaaba, the holy black stone on which Abraham is believed to have prepared the sacrifice of Isaac.

A Muslim religious commandment held that persons of means should, in commemoration of Abraham's sacrifice, slaughter sheep on Id el Adha and distribute their meat among the poor. Weeks before the feast, sheep were being fattened in pleasurable anticipation of that great event, and Cairo would come to resemble one huge manger, with the doleful bleating of the victims reverberating from virtually every rooftop and every back yard—even from the front stairs of posh buildings, where they were held tethered to the banisters. My father, an agnostic, reacted to all this excitement with mordant irony, though he was prevented from expressing his views on the subject outright by my mother, who, as soon as he opened his mouth, would cut him off, exclaiming, "Darling, please! Not in front of the children!" Her own attitude was that all religions were good: the main thing was to have one; and she did justice to her creed, whenever I was expelled from school, by following up her visit to the Muslim holy shrine of Saida Zeinab, with one to the church of St. Theresa—a Christian friend having vouched that that lady worked miracles. But my aunt, a devout Muslim, frowned on these equivocations; she always insisted that my mother bring us every year to her farmhouse so we would learn our traditions. (She considered the fact that I preferred less sanguinary forms of pastimes, such as searching out the colored Easter eggs hidden in my friend Anne-Marie's garden or looking for gingerbread men under her Christmas tree, as just one more example of my "mental corruption" by the West.)

Out of noblesse oblige, it was customary for the landlord and his family to preside over the slaughter of the sheep and the distribution of the meat (to this day my cousin, now an eminent scientist, who has been converted to vegetarianism by Guru Krishna of Kerala, to whose ashram in southern India he makes biannual pilgrimages, feels duty-bound to keep up the tradition on the farm, which he has inherited from his parents). The sight of these creatures in convulsions, long after their heads had been severed from their trunks, of those large, soft, innocent, stupefied eyes with brains and blood oozing all over them, of those bodies which were being excitedly hacked to pieces by the peasants—the choicer parts going to those with large families; the other peasants having to content themselves with a tail, a foot, a belly, a head, whatever they could grab—always made me want to run away and cry. Only the fear of being called a sissy by my cousin kept me glued to my spot, looking on with fascinated horror at this gruesome scene: the peasants uttering little gleeful cries as their axes dug into their victims; the animals standing silently, without making a move to avoid the blows, watching, as off came their limbs, one by one, until their bodies caved in and out came their entrails. Then the head toppled over and rolled onto the sodden ground, where it lay with its eyes open, staring hard at you, until one of the ragged, barefoot children, who had been dancing joyfully on the smooth carpet of dark blood, picked it up and ran off with it to the village to offer to his mother.

By the end of the meal, Alex and I had both attempted several topics of conversation, not because we were interested in them but to avoid a certain topic neither of us dared broach. For once, the giggles that had always rescued us from a serious response to the world failed to come to our assistance. When silence had begun to weigh on us, Alex proposed to read my cup of Turkish coffee for me. He shook up the dregs in my cup three times, as custom called for, and turned the cup upside down on its small saucer. Then, pretending to study the sides of the cup intently, as the coffee grounds dried into all manner of lines and curves, he told me he saw a tall, blond man waiting for me on the other side of the ocean. He winked at me, but I was not amused. So he grabbed hold of my elbow and gave it a squeeze. "Seriously," he said, "it couldn't possibly work." He'd always known that one day he'd have to give me up, give me back to my own class, my own kind. "We're not the same race. Besides, I'm not the marrying sort. You must forget me."

I got up without answering him: I could only answer with my tears, and it would not do to cry in public. "*Ciao*," I said lightly, my face averted.

He looked up and, noticing my eyes brimming over, took hold of my arm and turned me gently toward him, brushing my cheek with his lips. I took the kiss and left, just like that, with the feel of his hand light and momentary upon my behind as if he were telling me, "Run along now, be a good girl, I need to be alone to think."

I walked past the milling crowds, down the long, tamarind-lined avenues. The crowds here were like nowhere else in the world. They were typical Egyptian crowds: the people moved slowly, patiently, lethargically, aimlessly, without curiosity, just going this way rather than that, in this city of fourteen million, probably the densest in the world. A colony of beggars had taken refuge under the 6th of October Bridge, built by Sadat to commemorate the "victory" over Israel in the 1973 war, which led to Mohandesin, a new residential district of fine houses for the *nouveaux riches*. The beggars were setting themselves up for the night, rolling out their torn mats, arranging their paraffin stoves and little naphtha lamps, fencing in their places with soiled cardboard boxes. Their children romped about in the dirt: babies whose diseased eyes already told of the ravages of dust and flies—small, sticky, tenacious flies; little boys, their bald skulls covered with festering sores, chasing verminous dogs; little girls, their kinky hair full of blood, of ticks, selling lottery tickets. They pushed against me as I passed, whispered to one another; sometimes they stopped to stare at me. The stares of hungry people always made me uneasy. I tried to disengage myself. I began to elbow my way forward, squeezing in and out of the empty spots along the sidewalks until I reached the Kasr el Nil Bridge. Then I ran down to the imposing buildings that carried the reassuring names of my childhood: Park Lane, Dorchester, Nile View.

By the time I reached home, I had begun to think that this journey which I was about to embark on was a blessing in disguise. At first I reasoned that I must understand Alex; he was, after all, older than me, he was sated, perhaps even wearied by experiences and pleasures that made it harder for him to love. But in the end, I gave in to my pique. I decided that though Alex might look like a god and have the charm of a prince, he was simply a petty, selfish, manipulative, empty person; that if the truth were told, the only meaningful words we ever exchanged were our cries to each other in the dark. Alex was right: I must give him up, give him back to his own class, his own kind, his own race.

I would go away and forget the stifling little flat across the bridge, with the tattered green wallpaper, forget the balcony with the soiled straw mat, on which we slept with Agrapimou on hot nights, forget the ugly scullery with the sink that smelled like a latrine, forget the staircase with the ragged rat holes. Yes, I felt quite sure that I would forget this place of distress, forget his face, his very name.

But I did not forget him. Many times in the misery of our separation I tried to free myself of my love for Alex by analyzing it away, by telling myself that Alex was a cad, a fake, a weakling, a coward—a Greek antihero, in short, and yes, a homosexual! But what was I trying to prove to myself by all that? I finally had to accept that my disillusionment with him was a pose. Far from fading with absence, my longing for him grew. The variety of his moods, by turn gay and melancholy, garrulous and taciturn, amiable and irascible, appealed to my instinct: I conjured up his image with all the force of desire. I saw my life slipping away in the stifling, airless stacks of Widener Library. I began to write to him, casually at first, then urgently. And I began to wait. Oh! that agonizing daily wait for the mailman, for that letter which carried up to me from Egypt, across frozen New England, into my Harvard carrel that scent which I instantly recognized, the sunny, hyper-distilled scent of citrus! I thought of him with a sentimental pang as I sat reading his letter by the dim light of the dusty lamp, and suddenly I found myself so longing for him that I went all the way to Harvard Square to buy a bottle of Egoïste. Finally, I returned to Egypt.

10

A HOUSE BY THE SHADOWY WATERS

THE UNIVERSITY had closed down for the Christmas vacation and Alex and I spent a few delightful days in Alexandria, despite the bleak winter weather, walking arm in arm down the rain-swept corniche; past the wharf where the old timbers of the ships groaned with every fresh assault of the winds—chilly winds which for us were like a warm embrace—past the little stands with the roasting chestnuts, whose coals glowed through the sea spray. And we laughed as we dodged a sudden splash of water from a passing car, on our way to Nouzha, the rose garden. Never had the oleanders, naked in the cold December afternoon, witnessed such a burst of confidences, so many stolen kisses!

In this manner we would stroll about idly until we noticed that the stars had begun to glimmer in the darkening sky. Drifting together down remembered streets —rue Pasteur, rue Suarès, rue des Soeurs, rue Nebi Daniel, rue du Musée—we saw, not the Alexandria that had turned into a mere shabby, provincial Mediterranean seaport, but the one that was inhabited by our memories.

All at once, altogether, the streetlights would have come on; there would be little pools of rainwater under the gas lamps, whose tremulous, smudged phosphorescence lit up here a solitary couple, there a man's furtive smile, a passing car, a whore along the seafront. Almost imperceptibly, the squares would empty of people, the trolleys would become fewer and fewer, till there would be no movement at all save the stealthy stalk of a stray dog crossing the tracks.

So we would return to Pension Corail, run by a certain Madame Rose, a voluble Armenian, full of expansive bonhomie, after warming our frozen bones with a bowl of *avgolemono* soup at one of the innumerable Greek tavernas that lined the shore. Sitting in the back of an old horse-drawn carriage, under its bright awning festooned with copper hands against the evil eye, we would watch the waves flailing against the rocks, tossing up clouds of foam, and the long, flowing strip of the corniche dissolving in the evening mist. Alex would let his hand rest on mine, moving his eyes to where my eyes went, allowing them, when the carriage passed something picturesque, to meet my own, smiling to signal to me that he was aware I found it charming and that he did, too—almost as much as I. It pleased me to think that he still had delighted attention to spare for the sparrows on the steeples of St. Mark's, the green dimness of the Antoniadis Gardens, with their classical Greek statues, the juggler of flaming torches outside the Atheneos. Every so often, I would order the jarvey to pull to a stop, for no reason other than my unhurried enjoyment of the city. Once we reached our little pension, we would step out onto the little balcony of our bedroom overlooking the sea, for one last good-night kiss under the brilliant moonlight.

When the weather was particularly bad, we would nestle on the flowery cretonne couch, next to Alex's sleeping cat, and sip *sahlab*, a winter drink of hot milk flavored with resin, as we listened to the soothing hush of the rain on the sea. Dreamily, delightfully, the hours would slip by until the mauve clouds of dusk would begin to float past us, daubing the houses with pastels, softening their outlines, settling on rooftops. We would keep on sitting by the open window, through which came the crackling of dilapidated horse carriages, as they slid through the slimy street below, until we heard the last tired horse clopping listlessly about his errand. Then we knew it was time for us, too, to turn in.

The next morning, we'd be awakened by the buzzing of the flies contentedly hatching on our windowsill. A speechless delight would take hold of us at the sight of the sun pouring into our bedroom. Outside, the colorful small boats—schooners, brigantines, caïques—would still be shimmering with dew, but the bright children's kites would already have begun to take the wind, and at the Automobile Club, across the street from us, little rich girls would be learning the crawl, in a pool carved into the rocks.

And so even in the winter, in our little pension room with the creaky wooden shutters, buffeted by the harsh desert winds, we felt the strange hold of this city bordered by the cold, acid-green waters of the sea, on the one side, and the metallic sheen of Mareotis, the salt lake, on the other.

When the time came to return to Harvard, I begged my parents to allow Alex to visit me in Boston for Easter. Since he was born in April, I had come up with the idea of offering him the ticket as a birthday present. Though I had not broached the subject directly with him—he cringed at the mere mention of that hemisphere—I sensed his secret yearning to go and his constant struggle with his rebellious desire. (Alex's secret fantasy upon entering our service had been that once Father's hip healed, he would accompany him as his personal attendant on his summer trips to Europe. He dreamed of the swanky cruise ship that would offer him the enjoyment of good deck chairs, native crews, and the distinction of being white.)

So one morning I sprang the idea on Mother.

"What! Are you mad? What about your father!"

"What of Father? The old man is in splendid shape."

"Isn't he." She took me up eagerly. "Still, one never knows."

I didn't answer. I'm afraid, I thought to myself, that if something were to happen to him, it would not be altogether a bad thing. Then Alex would be free to come at last, and what's more, he could stay as long as he liked, which would be just compensation for all his years of privation. But I did not share these thoughts with

Mother, who would have found them criminal. I went, instead, to look for Father.

I found him in his usual place, sitting perfectly erect in his unyielding chair, beside the small inlaid coffee table, holding his fly whisk with the long ebony handle inlaid with seed pearls in his initials—bearing it rigidly the way one might bear a scepter.

There was something intimidating about this solemn, almost hieratic, figure, whose feet rested on a handsome damask footstool. Still, I plucked up my courage and presented the case for Alex's departure: his devotion in my father's service—surely he deserved some reward; his inability to afford vacations in the past; the astounding fact that he'd hardly ever set foot outside Egypt; what a marvelous opportunity this would be for him, his only chance to travel, perhaps. And how quickly he'd be back—two weeks was, after all, such a short time.

My father listened attentively to my moving little speech. When I had finished, he raised his coffee cup and took a few nonchalant sips, forcing me to wait helplessly for an interminable moment before his immobile eyes. At last he pronounced himself. In a dry, imperious tone, he told me that I should leave the matter of the "servants'" vacations to my mother. I should not interfere.

I could see it was pointless to try to pursue further the dialectic of our relative positions, yet for a second I lingered, looking at that impassive, rocklike face, at the pale cold eyes. It was hard for me to recognize in this furious wreck the fine old figure of the magnanimous, playful father I had once known. Suddenly I felt an overpowering urge to get away from that stern, implacable presence, that dismal, barren house, that airless, shuttered room impregnated with the smell of his rank flesh, of his 4711 cologne and his urinal, of that camphor-reeking fur shawl that had once been used to warm the knees of his uncle, the Prime Minister, Rushdi Pasha, in his horse-drawn carriage.

I returned to Egypt in early March. Claiming a family problem, I had asked for a leave of absence. The range of color is extraordinary in Egypt at that time of year, when the plants are coming into tenderest leaf—pale lime, dark indigo, deep emerald—and the air is sweet with the odor of hidden orange groves and budding jasmine blooms.

Perhaps the sole bad omen was the ponderous black clouds that the sky was unrolling; they threatened to fill the cities with dust as the sandstorms hailing from the desert swirled and swept across the plains, filtering into the houses, coating the furniture, abrading clothes, choking the drains, invading everything. There is no real spring in Egypt, no renewal, because of these sandstorms—only the long, monotonous hot months, which follow the short, chilly winters.

I had many enchanting afternoons in Alex's flat, ate simple fare cooked over a small gas Primus stove and drank out of *ulas*, porous earthenware jars that keep water cool, for Alex had no refrigerator. He stored several of them on the floor under the iron sink in the scullery, and when, as often happened, there was no water in the faucet because a pipe had burst, we used them for bathing, too. He liked to wallow up to his neck in the water, which I had boiled with discarded lime and orange peel, and to inhale their perfumes. So soothing were they to him, he sometimes dozed off, his head resting against the edge of the big red plastic washtub, his legs sticking out the other end. I would wake him by tickling his neck with kisses and then I would soap him, beginning with his hair, ears, and neck, and would splash him with cool water from the *ula*. He would shiver, making clattering noises with his teeth, and we would laugh. After the bath was over, he would have me sprinkle his body, profusely, with his cologne. He adored that. For even in the past, when Alex had fallen on hard times, had starved in his dank apartment or turned to friends for charity meals, he had always somehow found the money for Egoïste. His skin, clothes, personal effects, the entire house was saturated with it. And he left a telltale citrus-scented trail behind him wherever he went.

Finally, it would be the floors' turn. We would squat on our knees and, using the same soap we had just used on ourselves, begin with the scullery floor, where we had bathed in the washtub, and gradually work our way through the rest of the apartment, pouring the filthy water down a slimy drain in the balcony, from which it splattered onto the caked mud down below. When we were done, the whole house had a delicious smell of purity and respectability. Alex would revel in it. He would haul out his old phonograph to celebrate, and we would dance naked, cheek to cheek, to the tune of one of his favorite Barbara records:

Apparu, disparu,
L'homme en habit rouge.
Dis-moi, dis-moi, d'où viens-tu?

Appearing, disappearing,
Man in red.
Tell me, tell me, where have you come from?

Alex's skin had the softness of rose petals, the fruity smell of perfume. I cuddled closer in his arms as we circled around the floor. We would finish off the dance in bed: his tongue was expert, marvelous. I would close my eyes on the intense pleasure.

Once, when we were ensconced among the lilac-colored down pillows that lined Alex's bedstead, and Alex was reading to me an old British mystery story, out of one of the secondhand books he purchased from the sidewalk bookstalls of the Ezbekiya Gardens, there came the quick, light patter of footsteps on the staircase and, looking over his shoulder, I saw what seemed like the lean silhouette of a man on the frosted glass panel of the main door. At that very moment the sound of a key fumbling in the lock caused Alex to look up, and seeing the direction of my glance, he turned his head. He must have guessed that it was his Danish lover, because he quickly pulled a sheet over us and slipped a protective arm over my shoulder. Had his friend come in, he would have found us in this ridiculous pose, like two children caught in a naughty prank in a school dormitory. But as it happened, his friend seemed to hesitate: perhaps he had heard the tail end of Alex's unfinished sentence and guessed that someone was with him (though he must have thought it was someone of the male sex). We saw the figure recede and heard the footsteps once again, this time growing fainter and fainter, until at last, giving vent to a flood of relief, we burst out laughing.

These simple pleasures, these precious moments of exhilarating freedom, gave us the fortitude to bear our golden cage for yet another week.

On weekends we sometimes managed to get away to our home in Sidi Kreir. We spent rapturous hours there, luxuriating in its simplicity, reveling in the sheer joy of being together. As soon as we arrived, we would take ourselves for long strolls along the seashore, until at the end of the day we would drop down, exhausted, onto the sand, following the sinking sun's course through half-closed lids, as we let our skins absorb its last pale rays. We would lie on in the dark exchanging unhurried kisses, under a sky full of falling stars, listening to the rumble of the waves, the sea receding, gathering, and returning in its immensity. In love, Alex may have given little because he had no self to give, but in pleasure, he gave the whole world—he was warmer, gentler, stronger, than the currents that caressed our naked bodies.

Once as we were walking back home in the still, moonlit night, I felt Alex's arm tighten about my shoulders, and looking up, I caught sight of his exhilarated face: directly overhead, the sky was laced with streamers of wild geese fleeing the heat, returning to the cooler climes of Europe.

Untroubled, unhurried, the days moved onward, brilliantly sunny days that made everything appear bathed in color. Whereas before my departure for the United States I had had the feeling that if my affection delighted Alex at times, at other times he bore it with weary resignation, since my return he seemed full of tender solicitude and concern, such as one might lavish on a person one has feared one has lost. He used terms of endearment when he addressed me that I had never heard him use before; and sometimes he held my hands in his while he spoke to me, looking into my eyes with such tenderness as to make me blush. His whole personality seemed to be changing: gone was his caustic irony; in its place had come a tone reflective, mellow, full of sad sobriety.

One afternoon, as we sat sipping mango juice on our

patio in Sidi Kreir, Alex offered to drive me down to Lake Mareotis the following morning, to visit his friend Pano's house. I was overjoyed, because I had long wanted him to show it to me, yet heretofore my pleas had fallen on deaf ears.

The thrill of anticipation must have exhausted me. That night I remember dropping heavily onto my mastaba and feeling the cool air, sharp with the salty brine of the sea, stroking my cheeks. When I awoke, the stars were shining on my face through the wrought-iron windows, and Alex lay curled up in a ball next to me, snoring heavily. From somewhere unseen the melancholic notes of a *qasida* floated in; a Bedouin was singing the traditional complaint of unrequited love—a song full of the wild heartsickness of the desert. Soon the marvelous spring night cast its spell on me, too, and I felt myself dozing off once more. But during my sleep the sweetness and peace of the evening gave way to the howling of pariah dogs slinking about Bedouin encampments, to the shrieking of cocks, and to the moaning of quails trapped in the cages, camouflaged with reeds, that had been set out to snare them.

The next day we awoke at sunrise; from where we lay, only the mauve haze of the desert horizon was visible.

We sped through whirls of dust, on the desert road, past thundering open trucks bearing grim-faced soldiers with legs planted wide apart and trousers flapping hard, until we reached a narrow path and began to wind our way slowly uphill around the sand dunes, whose olive trees, bathed in the cold light of dawn, appeared speckled with waves of tiny bells. We crossed a flat strip of sand dotted with date trees and began to ascend once more. By the time we got to the top of the darkened hills, the skies were already turning a purplish brown, which presaged the gathering of a sandstorm somewhere in the desert. Then slowly they began to darken, until by sunset they were swelling with huge black clouds ready to unload their heavy burden of dust upon Egypt's cities and villages.

How startlingly the landscape changed now! How wild, almost biblical, it appeared, with its gnarled old trees, the yellow-blossomed acacias and the red-blossomed pepper trees, which had been planted by Egypt's foreign residents to lure the migratory birds, and its all too vivid orange sand bordered by a thread of inky black—Lake Mareotis, visible for the first time.

At the edge of the lake were the deserted mansions with their swimming pools, which glimmered in the dim light like mirages. These houses had clearly fallen on evil days, yet from a distance a certain air of desolate splendor seemed to pervade them despite the dilapidated masonry, the empty pools with the rusty generators, and the overgrown tennis courts.

At last we turned onto a dusty road; the abandoned trails leading to the hunting lodges were now detectable. Spokes of darkness reached out to us from the lake, which was still groggy with the inertia of the sleeping desert: in the heavy marsh mists it seemed full of evanescent figures.

Alex and I got out of the car to stretch our legs. Leaning against a pepper tree, he lit himself a cigarette. He glanced absently at the distant mansions, seemingly reconciled to their ruin. No sadness touched him.

When we got back into the car, we noticed white drifts of sand had begun to infiltrate it. Soon the wind gathered strength; we could hear the harsh, sobbing air outside as we drove on, and from time to time, we caught a glimpse of the ghostly figures of Bedouin men—their faces shrouded in white kerchiefs—shuffling past us in groups of three and four, silent as death itself.

The giant dust clouds that had amassed in the Delta began to drift toward the salt lake in great dark columns resembling pillars of smoke, and we observed how the sand settled into the lake.

In the end we were forced to abandon our car. As we haltingly advanced down the twisting narrow path along the mud embankment lined with palm groves and black swamps, we could feel the sand weighing down our eyelids, scorching our throats and nostrils, parching our lips, cracking our skin.

At last Alex pointed out to me a garden where the trees nodded their dusty fronds. As we got closer, I saw it surrounded a rambling old mansion. The slats of the Venetian blinds were coated with white powder, for the sand had slowly been invading everything in the large, shuttered rooms: clothes, books, cutlery, pictures long locked away and forgotten—everything.

Pushing open an unhinged gate, we walked past a row of dead trees toward a portico, opening onto an outside terrace. Its stairs were slippery with animal excrement. A scorpion lurked in a crack of the banister. Alex looked at it indifferently, as though it were only natural that it should be there to greet us. At my expression of fear, he shrugged his shoulders, saying that the surrounding desert was full of them and that when the Europeans first settled near Lake Mareotis they used to put bowls of water under the feet of the bed in order not to get bitten in their sleep. We roamed about the large house silently, in a desultory fashion, past cool, dusty rooms crowded with the huge carcasses of Queen Anne furniture—rooms that had not been looted because the Bedouins, the sole inhabitants of this desert area, still lived in unfurnished tents as their fathers and forefathers had done before them. There was something stale and moribund about these rooms that made them appear tomb-like. But Alex steered me through them with the air of an impassive tour guide in a museum.

We reached a large kitchen, which Alex told me had once been the amphitheater where, during the grand festivities, four cooks, their sweating black faces capped by flowery-white turbans, and twelve *soufragis*, their caftans divided at the waist by crimson sashes, their hands cased in white gloves, played out their roles. There were the wild birds their masters had shot down, which had to be laid out on long, gilded platters, stuffed with chestnuts and crowned with tufts of feathers; there were the cakes which had to be decorated with the candied purplish-blue scarabs, the emblem the Greek family had chosen for itself; there were masses of roses, chrysanthemums, gladioli, poppies, and cyclamen, freshly plucked from the garden, which had to be arranged in different-sized vases; there was the silverware which had to be taken out and polished till it shone. A special meal had to be prepared for the Greek musicians, who would arrive before the guests, toting their bouzoukis, and would, after they had eaten in the kitchen, take up their places on the open-air terrace, where there would later be dancing, carefully pulling out their black tails from underneath them, as they sat down, so they wouldn't get crumpled. After the banquet was over, a whole day would be spent cleaning up after the guests, checking the carpets for wine spots, counting the silver to make sure nothing had been stolen by the servants, throwing out the wilted flowers, putting away the shimmering goblets in the armoire and the embroidered tablecloths and china in the glossy dining room sideboards.

The kitchen windows overlooked the tennis courts in back of the house, from which every afternoon the twang of rackets had once been heard, for Alex and Pano invariably played a game while the grownups napped. I stole a sidelong glance at Alex, who was surveying the courts from the back porch. That handsome, impossibly handsome, impenetrable Greek face . . .

After a moment, he seemed to remember I was with him, for his hand reached out in search of mine. I smiled at him, looking directly into his eyes, eyes that did not quite return my smile, though his mouth suggested one. He led me up to his friend's bedroom on the second floor to show me the handsome old-fashioned canopied bed, with the matching rosewood lowboy, and the William and Mary secretary, where Pano had sat to do his homework. The shelves above the writing table still held a two-volume work on the history of the ancient Greeks and an illustrated book of Greek mythology, as well as a whole row of notebooks, filled with his crabbed writing, going back to primary school. Alex led me out to an evil-smelling small chapel, where Pano and his mother had prayed every morning. Birds perched on some Greco-Roman columns behind it, which had been transplanted into an immense and now weed-filled garden: they cast terrifying shadows, in the half-light, onto a pool covered with green scum, whose desolate springboard hung by a rotting clamp.

I was eager to leave by then and could not understand why Alex lingered broodingly over the place. But he seemed intent on showing me one last thing. So I followed him to the little wooden hut where he and his friend would undress before their game of tennis. He seemed surprised to find some clothes still there, including a navy school blazer, with a gold badge, left hanging on a peg. And for the first time his face betrayed some sign of emotion: dismay at the stench of musk emanating from Pano's once crisp tennis flannels and at the greenish stains that capped the toes of his friend's molding white sneakers.

As we left through the back door leading out of the servants' quarters, we could see pariah dogs prowling about the deserted horse stables. The sandstorm made them restless; they howled like beings in pain. We hastened away, almost afraid to look back lest we ourselves turn into pillars of sand, for we had the impression that everything we were leaving behind—the stables, swimming pool, tennis courts, gardens, chapel, mansion, everything, in short, that had once formed Europe in Egypt—was destined to be obliterated by the khamsin, carried off by a final eddy into the great salt lake, where it would vanish once and for all.

All the way back, we could hear the wind raging outside the car windows, unpacking the vast desert, ransacking it, now piling the fine sand particles into white mounds, beautiful as cloudscapes, now scattering them, eradicating them. How eerie it felt to discover on reaching Sidi Kreir that our spring had been buried by a sliding sand dune.

A subtle change came over Alex following our return: he lapsed into long, distracted silences, musing over his past as though everything he had experienced in his childhood and had forgotten or chosen to repress had been condensed into the visual memory of that single, powerful emotional moment at the lake site. Soon the shadow of his discontent began to creep into our relationship. When I tried to revive the old raptures that had always accompanied our stay in Sidi Kreir, he responded at first with delight, but after a brief spell, he lapsed back into a depression so deep that it seemed as though nothing in the world would be able to pull him out of it.

I realized that my belief in our total identification with each other was an illusion, that somehow the happiness we always experienced in this isolated, idyllic setting had kept me from seeing him as a person who, like myself, lived on many different levels simultaneously, and that there were whole areas of his life which he still kept hidden from me, secrets which he had not revealed to me. Had he succumbed to loneliness, to the haunting memory of this old, shadowy house on the edge of the dark, reed-fringed waters? Or did this agony to which he could not give expression have something to do with the nature of his relationship with Pano? I sensed that the key to this enigma might lie there, but when I questioned him about it he answered me irritably or not at all.

This new self, this ill-tempered, morose version of his old self, he kept from others—he never, in fact, radiated such calculated charm in front of my parents as when we returned to Cairo. His company was as sought after as ever; the same old bores continued to flock to our house day in and day out in hopes of seeing him. Not once did he betray his inner struggle in public; only I sensed the anxiety behind that handsome, indolent mask he proffered to others: an anxiety whose roots lay far back in the past, further back than I, or perhaps even he, could grasp.

11

EGYPT LOST AND RECOVERED

THEN ALEX FELL SICK. For three days he lay on his cot, his eyes closed, looking very pale. Once or twice I thought I saw his lips quiver and his teeth clench, but he never said anything to me about the images behind his eyes, never spoke of his pain. Father complained of his groans at night, which disturbed his sleep. So, on the third day, Mother called an ambulance: she claimed he would get better care in the hospital. Alex did not want to go. I wept when they came to take him away, wept without letting anyone see my tears, because Alex was just *un misérable Grec*, as Mother said, and one ought not to weep for a miserable Greek.

At first I stayed away from him. He had told my sister he did not want me to see him in this condition. I waited for his news in an agony of impatience. My sister went to see him every day, took him the bottle of Egoïste and the silk dressing gown I had bought him, our radio, a *Paris Match*—whatever he requested. And she brought back a report that a kind, portly old Greek doctor was taking care of him, that he would call out every morning, "*Yassou, palikari mou*"—hello, my brave young man—and Alex, delighted with this complimentary form of address, would show off his Greek repertoire. That she had found Alex sulking because he did not care for the food and that the nurses, who doted on him, turned their heads when she smuggled him the baklavas he craved—even though they were strictly against doctor's orders. Then the depressing news that Alex's liver ailment had worsened, his stomach was swollen and distended, and the doctor spoke of draining out the water, which he feared would get into his lungs, but Alex would not hear of it. He did not want to be left with a scar on his belly. His Danish lover had surfaced one morning and had stood outside in the corridor and cried. He would not return, he said: he could not bear to see Alex like this. All kinds of distant relatives had crept out of the woodwork and begun to visit him in the hope of being remembered in his will. Even the cousin from Greece had arrived to lay claim to his flat, which she wanted to use as a pied-à-terre during her visits to Egypt.

Deprived of seeing him, I sought out the comfort of his house. The evenings had become bitter to me now; I feared them in advance. The darkness on Antiquity Street, with its vista of stunted black houses, crowded together, its dim streetlamps and its street cats, who suddenly, out of nowhere, darted screaming across one's path, seemed full of foreboding.

I plodded through the old quarter, taking in the hot fragrance of jasmine in the narrow, sleeping lanes and the occasional murmur of voices that escaped the open windows. Slowly I made my way up the stairs, followed by a lame dog—the only commiserating soul, it appeared, willing to minister to my solitude. I crossed the threshold of Alex's apartment, that irrevocable demarcation, driven by a nervous longing to find the imprint of his body on the rumpled bed, the shape of his head on the awry pillow, the arch of his feet on the spotted rubber mat, those slender, bare feet with the delicate toenails, exactly as I had seen them the first time, motionless, the curve of the bed rising just beyond them. But the things that would have reminded me of his presence—his fine silk shirts, which he used to iron meticulously and store in a closet packed with mint leaves (according to Alex, a mouse repellent), his elegant jackets, his flamboyant scarves, his rings and bracelets—anything worth taking had vanished. His cousin, it seemed, had visited the flat before me to claim his puny legacy.

The bare room had about it a quiet, static quality that made it colder than any living cold. But I bore the cold, bore it with a sort of guilty misery, returning to the room night after night to throw myself onto the bed—that nuptial bed of love and grief—where I could give vent freely to my tears.

I cannot even begin to describe the vertiginous excitement that took hold of me when at last he sent for me: I could feel myself shake as I made my way down the long hospital corridor in search of his room. I had a moment of doubt and apprehension as I stood there gazing at this supine figure: he was so much thinner than I remembered, and his hair was shockingly gray. (I realized with a start that his hair must always have been dyed.) Recognizing him dimly through his disguise, I told myself that this must be he, that it was indeed my old friend. Alex!

I think he felt the force of my recognition pressing upon him because he opened his eyes and, noticing my frozen stare, reached out for the bed rails, letting out a sigh that sounded like the exhalation of a lifetime of slow, heat-laden time.

For a while he lay thus, his frail, outstretched arms clutching the rails. I found intact amid this wreckage the lovely blue of his eyes, which a halo of fatigue had enlarged: they loomed in the dark against the pallor of his face, full of baffled, pathetic incomprehension. He evidently could not understand what he was doing so far away from his youth in a stifling hospital room redolent of cemetery flowers. I, too, just sat there in uncomprehending silence. My tongue, paralyzed by my contact with a reality so different from anything I had imagined, could not formulate words of comfort. This wraithlike being was a stranger to me; I dared not touch him, dared not kiss his wan, haggard face or caress his emaciated body, dared not even look at him for fear he would notice how diminished I found him.

He must have sensed my confusion, for he asked me why I looked so pale. "It's the heat," I said, "it's suffocating in this room!"—turning my head away from him so he would not notice I had begun to cry.

But the next day he already looked better, having used the ash-blond hair dye I brought him. And I half expected him to bound out of bed the moment I entered the room, as he used to do in the old days when he woke up from his siesta, imperiously clamoring for his lemonade and his hot bath water with the infusion of citrus peel.

Only one incident stands out in the days that followed. Once, as we were engaged in small talk, we heard the clang of the tin cups of a licorice-juice vendor, a shrill sound that cut across our flow of words. Alex stopped right in the middle of a sentence, his face contracted, and I guessed that that sound had brought up a rush of memories: memories of a life that was no longer his, of his favorite alleys in his neighborhood, of the thick smell of spices, of the taste of Oriental pastries, of his jocular exchanges with the street peddlers—of all those things, in short, which had provided him with the simplest, surest pleasures. And perhaps he realized that now nothing was left to him but to watch the slowly changing colors of the sky from his hospital bed, as the day moved into night.

In an attempt to comfort him, I began to talk about

America, about how he must join me there after his convalescence, how we would live there together.

A disdainful look suffused his delicate profile.

"What is it?" I asked, stretching out an arm across the bed rail to take his hand in mine. "Don't you trust me?"

"You!" he said, pointing at me and breaking into harsh, jeering laughter. "You're a nut! You'll walk out on me just as you did on your husband."

I didn't answer him. I merely got up and left, recognizing that his words were not really addressed to me. They were part of a long internal argument. He simply could not believe that finally someone had come along who valued him solely for himself. Like a gambler, he was afraid to stake everything on a turn of the wheel.

At last the good news: he was out of danger. The doctor spoke of sending him home for Easter.

The joy I felt was like nothing else. It overwhelmed me, made me feel I loved everyone on earth. Heaven only knows how I mustered the will power to hold myself in check, to dissimulate, to keep myself from dashing out the door to the hospital and covering him with kisses the moment Mother brought the news home. It was precisely such an exhibition of emotion in front of the nurses that she feared. I should not forget that I was a pasha's daughter. Everyone knew it. What would people say if they saw me. For heaven's sake, no need to let the whole world in on your sordid little affair. *"Surtout pas de scandale, je t'en supplie!"* (Above all, no more scandal, I beg of you!)

Somehow I managed to counterfeit a walk of slow piety as I gathered a few fruits and magazines to take to him.

Apparu, disparu,
L'homme en habit rouge.
Dis-moi, dis-moi, d'où viens-tu?

How long had it been since I had caught myself humming like this? An eternity? It was not just my relief: this pathetic refrain helped me recover his magical image, which I had lately tried to erase from my memory in preparation for the inevitable.

In a matter of days, Alex felt sufficiently heartened by the good news to make plans. We were to be wed in the hospital, secretly, because in Egypt it was forbidden for Muslim women to marry Christians. Alex, who, since he took to his bed, had renewed his friendship with Père Joseph, the stern Protestant pastor, would ask him to convert me, and I should pay two men from the old-age home for the poor, affiliated with the Greek Hospital, to act as witnesses.

It was strange to see this man—who had apparently become my lover without volition or desire and who only a short time ago had taken my proposal that we stake out a life together in America in his usual passive, sardonic spirit—so bent on marriage that he would not even consider waiting till he was discharged. Had he been chastened by misfortune and the shortening time ahead of him? Had he come to understand that it was aging and disease he had to argue away, not me? I could not quite dismiss the thought that he clung to me now because he felt ambushed by death. Overnight he had, without warning, stumbled down the precipice of old age: he had no doubt lost his faith in his eternal youth.

It took all my powers of persuasion to convince him to wait till he joined me in the States before taking so momentous a step. After all, it was not quite the land of gold-paved streets that he liked to imagine: *le grand luxe pour tout le monde*, as he was fond of saying. He must try living there first and he must try living there *with me*. We had barely lived alone together. Why was the marriage ceremony so important all of a sudden? I asked him. Surely it was not the contract he was after, the very respectability of marriage, which I scorned and had therefore neglected to offer him when I suggested to him that he come live with me in the States?

I went on and on in this vein as one is wont to do when one feels one is lost in unknown territory and hopes to give one's arguments strength by repetition. Strangely, it was I who was now weighed down by the very same practical considerations that I had scornfully dismissed only a short while back when friends had entertained them.

Suddenly I felt hot and nervous: I pleaded fatigue and left. Outside in the street, the air was foul and stagnant, but it refreshed me, and I decided to take myself for a long walk across the city in order to try and resolve the sentimental problem that bothered me. Involuntarily, my feet retraced the path to Antiquity Street, and I found myself before a tattered, wretched man who stood up against a wall, peeing and whimpering under the brutal glare of a streetlamp. The small puddle that was forming around him glittered in the dark. I turned away from him and tried to lose myself in this huge tragic city, where unsuspected misery lurked beneath the dirty night. But there was no peace for me between the two currents that flowed in my nature: the passionate current, which assured me I should rest happy in the knowledge that Alex had come to care for me and that everything would work out fine because of the affection between us, and the rational current, which irksomely voiced the reservations I dared not voice aloud. What would Alex do once I was back at Harvard? Would he idle away his time as a kept man? How would he fit into my circle of snooty, intellectual friends in Cambridge? And afterward, what would become of him once I embarked on my precious career? Would he wash dishes or work in a supermarket?

I shamefully dismissed these thoughts as unworthy of the feelings we had for each other, feelings that I was sure would help us overcome all such obstacles. Still, I could not help wondering why I had not leaped at Alex's offer. Was it not what I had hoped for, prayed for, waited for? Why then, instead of being rapturously happy, did I feel so singularly depressed?

When the day of my departure arrived, I set out to say goodbye to Alex. He lay with his face turned toward the picture of the Virgin, which was flanked on one side by that of the Savior and on the other by that of Agrapimou, his cat (who had by then joined the Savior, having slipped off the balcony ledge and broken her neck; it was the only time I had seen Alex shed tears). From the croaking little snores emanating from Alex's half-open lips I gathered he was fast asleep, and I did not have the heart to wrench him away from the happy dream world he was perhaps now inhabiting, complete with his favorite saints and martyrs—for no doubt St. Lucy and St. Elmo were there, too. So I waited a little, letting my eyes rove all over him. He seemed vulnerable as he lay at the mercy of the unseen observer: the hair at the back of his head looked very thin, with the sweaty locks parting to reveal a pinkish scalp, and the skin of his neck was loose and wrinkled.

Feeling vaguely guilty at watching him in his sleep, I decided to wake him.

"Alex," I called out softly, trying to suppress the anxious quaver in my voice.

I began to talk to him with affected casualness about all the things we would do once he was well enough to join me in America. But I could tell by his sullen silence that he found it difficult to focus his attention on what I was saying. God, I prayed inwardly, don't let him bring up *that* subject again. Don't let him expect an answer from me now!

"Alex, listen to me," I implored. And I began to remind him how much *I, too*, had missed him, that I'd come from the States especially to see him. "And now it's—" I caught myself up short. My thoughts had been about to escape my control. We looked at each other, and a tacit confession passed and repassed between us.

"And now it's too late! You've come back and found an old man. Why don't you say so?"

"No! No!" I heard myself lying.

He gestured for me to stop and urged me, in a tone of pleading weariness that I had never heard before, to leave.

I hesitated for a moment, but seeing that he had turned his head away, and not knowing what more to say, I started for the door.

A rustle behind my back made me turn around. I was not mistaken: Alex had pulled the sheet back and was pushing something toward me—the ring that was swimming on his finger. I took it and brushed his stubby cheek with my lips. He uttered a short, dry sob disguised as a cough. And I ran off. Ran without turning to look at him, ran all the way home, clutching the cheap emerald with the wreath of tiny false diamonds, tears pouring down my face.

I forget the exact phrasing of my sister's letter, forget whether she used a euphemism to soften the blow or whether she merely laid out in plain language the brutal fact that he had died of sclerosis of the liver. I think she began her letter with the Arabic form of address: *Te 'ishi inti*, may you yourself have a long life, which is the Egyptian way of coating the bitter pill one is about to give someone to swallow. There was a fairly lengthy description of the "splendid" funeral he'd been given on a fine spring day . . . first the prayers for his soul in the little Orthodox church that lay within the compound of the Greek Hospital, then the burial ceremony in Alexandria in the lovely Christian cemetery with the magnolia trees, whose white blossoms rained on the graves. How as she stood there, in this quiet graveyard, listening to the sweet, sad warble of the birds, she thought of me and regretted I had not been able to see it all: the handsome rosewood coffin she had had made to order for him by the best (and most expensive!) carpenter in Cairo, an Italian by the name of Dell'arte, who liked to refer to himself as an *ébéniste*, a cabinetmaker, and the magnificent cross of white and purple dahlias she had ordered for his tomb. Why, I could not have done more for him myself! She had even gone especially early to the church to make sure candles were lit before the coffin arrived. She had been the only one at the service besides the Greek owner of the Hotel Apollo, where he had worked, and an elderly woman, visibly lower-class but nice, whom she had spotted a couple of times at the hospital, always accompanied by a basket of ducks richly festooned with layers of coagulated fat, deep-fried breaded lamb brains, grape leaves, and *mumbar*, a stuffed sheep's intestine, along with bottles of drinking water perfumed with orange-blossom and rose-petal essences, presumably to help Alex down these meals—all of which she would pull out from underneath her voluminous, black *milaya*, as soon as the nurse left the room, the way a magician would conjure up rabbits from under his sleeve. Finally, my sister spiced the letter with a little bit of gossip: the owner of the Apollo, who had known Alex since he was a boy, had insinuated that he was not nearly as young as he made himself out to be; word was that he was forty-nine years old at his death. And in a postscript my sister informed me that Alex had left his jewel chest with her, for me.

Alex dead. Dead. I read and reread the letter in a frenzy of despair, passion, and remorse. During the time in which I believed he had waited as I did, clinging to the hope I would bring him to the States—time in which I had existed in a state of apathy that was almost peace, leading the busy, dreary life of an academic whose sex had shriveled up and atrophied—he had, unknown to me, lain in the hospital, suffered, and died alone.

At first I felt only anger. Anger at myself for not having been with him. Anger at my parents, who had deprived Alex of his chance to come to the States, where I felt certain he would have received better medical care. Anger at my sister, for I did not believe her words of commiseration, her pious sentiments. No, I did not believe she could ever quite forgive this man who had one day, with the suddenness of a hurricane, entered her peaceful, uneventful family life, done irrevocable damage, and then just as suddenly vanished. Anger at the doctor: had he not assured us that Alex was out of danger, that he'd be sending him home for Easter? Had he not wholeheartedly endorsed the idea of a voyage to America, after his convalescence, as something that would do him good?

And then I felt a torrent of grief. And what grief! I had never grieved for anyone the way I grieved for Alex, and I will never grieve that much again. Never. I wanted to die of his death.

Two years later, I returned to Egypt for my father's funeral. By a cruel irony he, too, died in the spring, in the same month as Alex had. My sister telephoned to say he had died in five days of an internal hemorrhage.

I had not been back to Egypt since Alex had died. I simply could not bear to come home and face the empty chaise longue in the living room. My eyes darted instinctively toward it, but it had vanished. I noticed with chagrin and surprise that the whole room had undergone a metamorphosis: I looked in vain for some piece of clothing, some small knickknack that had once belonged to Alex, but there was nothing, no trace of his existence; not a single picture of the Virgin, not even the scent of his Cleopatras, his cheap Egyptian cigarettes, or his expensive French cologne.

As I stood there trying to reconstruct the image of the chaise longue from memory, my sister, who had followed the direction of my eyes, told me it had been moved to the maid's room. The maid's room! I cannot convey the horror that these words inspired in me. I rushed to Fatma's room. She now slept on the same uncomfortable chaise longue where Alex had once slept. I looked at it as if it had been defiled and tried in vain to recover the atmosphere of those long hot nights when Alex and I sat on the floor with our backs against it, whispering so Father wouldn't hear us. Alex would slip an arm around my shoulders, and with the other he would hold a Cleopatra, taking nonchalant puffs, occasionally bringing it up to my lips. But Alex had vanished, utterly vanished; those enchanting nights had vanished; Father, too, had vanished. It was as if none of it had ever been.

I attempted to force Alex back into the room by an act of will, to evoke a single one of those nights, to hypnotize my memory by repeating his name to myself, as in a trance. When this did not work, I stepped forward and, looking intently at the wretched chaise longue, softly called out "Alex," as though this word, if spoken audibly enough, would have the magical effect of making him burst in, trailing his citrus fragrance behind him. But it was my sister who answered me instead. She had brought me the long-forgotten jewel chest, which was my legacy but which I had not been anxious to claim, assuming it contained the trinkets he had earned for his "services."

I took it to my room and broke the lock open, for he had not left me a key. How to describe my surprise when the first thing that caught my eye was a picture of Alex as a young boy, his arm around a belly dancer! Who was she? What trail of slime had she dragged across Alex's pitiful, muddled life? I could not help feeling a bit jealous—peeved also at his having kept this side of his life a secret from me. To be sure, I knew that since he had been thrown out of his home, at sixteen, he had not always kept the best of company. It seemed likely that long ago he had studied his horoscope and concluded that his chances in life were not such as to permit him to get rich by honorable means. For after his father had thrown him out of the house, his choice had been either to snatch what he could from the street vendors' carts, in the Bulak vegetable market, or to make the rounds of the garbage pails of the hotels along the Nile's golden strip; either to ride the fenders of buses with the unwashed natives or to stand inside and hope he'd be able to jump off after making his hit—almost invariably he chose the last course, which, though riskier, was far less wounding to his pride.

And so I tried to shrug the picture off by telling myself that it should come as no surprise that Alex had been around. He had told me once that he had earned a commission procuring women for a rich acquaintance of my parents in Zamalik, a highly regarded physician. And, after all, why should his having been a pimp be any more disturbing to me than his having been a homosexual hooker? I put the picture away and went on sorting through the box. Pictures of Alex as a boy. Pictures of Alex as an adolescent in school. Faded snapshots of his father—the resemblance was striking! A tinted picture of Alex outside a church with a young girl in braids. His cousin! The one who had come from Greece to claim his apartment. There was something touching about that picture of early boyhood taken before that indefinable moment when his pristine self, tired of standing aside and watching his own moral degradation, had at last departed from him altogether. The candor of those innocent blue eyes, that beautiful direct look from under the high brows!

Behind those eyes I could see Alexandria, the Alexandria in which he grew up. The little streetcars he rode as a child clicking on rusty wheels past buildings pockmarked by the constant onslaught of the salty sea breeze, past rat-infested shacks and brothels, behind whose closed shutters teenage girls, freshly arrived from Naples and Athens, were being sold. The creaking old horse carriages with the gay awnings, slowly clambering up the Grande Corniche toward the small harbor, with its oily gray waters and its rocky shore, white with the discarded fluff of cotton cargoes. The sleek black Cadillacs swishing past the broad, flame-tree-lined avenue, past the chattering sparrows of St. Mark's, past the uproarious cotton exchange, bearing painted ladies in broad-brimmed straw hats, studded with flowers, from their stylish villas on rue de France and the Rond Point to the dressmaker, the chiropodist, the fortune-teller, and the open-air teahouse, Pastroudis, where maimed beggars bobbed up and down the sidewalk trying to catch the eyes of the paunchy, red-fezzed pashas and the lean European brokers in melon hats, who sat studying the figures in La Bourse Egyptienne and picking cake crumbs off pendulous bosoms.

Yes, I could see it all through his eyes, the beauty and crushing poverty of Alexandria. I could hear the murmur of the surf, the rattle of backgammon boards, the clip-clop of the horses' hooves and the crackling of the windswept palms flanking the Windsor Palace, the exquisite strains of the mandolin in Santa Lucia Restaurant and, outside, the sad, inane whine of the barrel organ with the performing monkey. I could detect the smell of *biscotti* in the Italian *pasticcerie* and of the waiters' sweaty armpits, the wondrously scented silk handkerchiefs of the Greek gentlemen in Taverna Diamantakis and the reek of their drink-sodden mouths, the whiffs of perfume shed by the nice Jewish girls of Pension Zion, and the musty odor of their hidden parts, which they opened up for plowing, mingling with the rank breath of their clients' coated tongues—all this captivating detail of color, sound, and scent which made Alexandria, the Alexandria of the past, of my past, of his past, so languorous, decadent, and fatal.

And what was this? Could this be Alex's identity card? It was Alex's picture all right, but the name? Ali Abd el Rahman. A Muslim name, an Egyptian I.D. What on earth was he doing with an Egyptian I.D.? *Paliathropo*, I whispered under my breath (a Greek equivalent of the "S.O.B." he often used). What kind of joke was he playing on me from beyond the grave?

I could not quite control the tremor of my hands as I rummaged among the documents, because I sensed the key lay there, in those jumbled pieces of jigsaw puzzle, waiting, almost lurking, ready to reveal to me Alex's whole life, his past, his childhood, the woman who was his mother.

A thin, yellowed envelope slipped to the floor, and I picked it up with a curious premonition. It contained some musty parchments, so thin they had become transparent with time and clung to one another like layers of onion peel. They were legal documents written out in longhand, in a flourishing old-fashioned script full of whirls and curves. Here, I hoped, I feared, was the answer.

I began to read, my fear deepening into a terror of what was coming next, for nothing is more dreadful than to explore the innermost secrets of a person one has loved and lost. The first of these parchments, which had a French copy appended to it, had been issued by the Greek consulate in Alexandria. It certified that on April 13, 1936, a baby in a wicker basket, with nothing but a name tag pinned to its swaddling clothes, had been found outside the front door of Mr. and Mrs. Nikolaides. Inquiries addressed by the Greek couple to the health authorities had led to the discovery that a male child by the name of Ali Abd el Rahman had indeed been delivered at the Moassat Hospital on that day. But all subsequent efforts on the part of the Nikolaideses to trace the parents had proved vain, and no one had stepped forward since to claim the child. This being the case, the Greek consulate was prepared to grant the request of the Nikolaideses that they be allowed to officially adopt the child, that he be given Greek nationality, and that he be registered at the consulate under his new name, Alexander Nikolaides.

I forced myself to study these documents with a sort

of painful academic precision, trying as best I could to distance myself from the subject matter, perusing the material as though it were not the story of my lover but some long-neglected file in a police archive, a case which had been abandoned before it had been closed.

The next parchment, written in French many years later by a lawyer, a certain Vasilakis, on behalf of Alex's adoptive father, began with the word *Maîtres*, Honorable Sirs, and went on to request that the court nullify the act of adoption on the grounds that it was contrary to Egyptian law, which stipulated that a Muslim was entitled to adopt a Christian child, since he would be bringing it within the fold of Islam, but no Christian could adopt a Muslim child. In granting legal recognition to the act of adoption and to the subsequent baptism and renaming of the child, the Greek consulate had overstepped its prerogative; the court was therefore under obligation to agree to the father's request that the boy, who had disgraced his family through moral turpitude, no longer be entitled to bear his name or to receive a share of his legacy.

Then there was a document filed on behalf of Alex, appealing the court decision to nullify his adoption (it was rejected), and a petition in Arabic addressed by Alex to the Ministry of the Interior, asking that he be allowed to go on using his Greek name, as he was not known to anyone under his real name. Finally, there was a form issued by the Ministry of War declaring that Ali Abd el Rahman had been exempted from army service on "health grounds," a certificate from his Greek elementary school, apparently, which I could not read, and a birth certificate listing his mother's name as Fatma Abd el Rahman, her age as eighteen, her nationality as Egyptian, and her religion as Muslim.

It seemed to me as I sat there on the floor, stunned by the revelation of the role Alex's real mother appeared to have played in his life, that I was at last beginning to understand what underlay the force of his contempt for the natives, the revulsion, almost venom, which animated him when he spoke of that "low race of people," those slow-witted, lazy, slovenly, cunning, untrustworthy Egyptians—and the tenacity with which he clung to his claim to racial superiority. Who was that wretched woman who had come to our house so long ago? I saw Alex's panic-stricken white face in a flash, the way he responded to the dressmaker's miserable embrace, that strange, furtive look, as though his fear of discovery, which he had tried in vain to suppress all these years, had suddenly been realized. And I remembered the look of savage resentment that passed over it the day I announced I had met an old school chum of his, and his question: "What did he tell you? Did he say I was an orphan?"

Only now did I understand that this incomprehensible fury went beyond the jealous rage at—and fierce yearning for—the mother, the hatred and vindictiveness against the father, that are the lot of every male child. I could not help feeling a little hurt in my vanity at discovering things this way, as I had liked to imagine that I was closer to him than anyone else: no one better able than I to understand how he had suffered at being scorned.

As I was brooding over these terrible documents, my eyes wandered once more in the direction of the pictures, which lay scattered. There was something peculiar about the hands of this belly dancer in the shimmering brassiere. And suddenly, as I studied her hands with their broad knuckles, it struck me that they were too big to be a woman's hands. Could this possibly be Pano, the Greek friend who had introduced him to duck shooting and perhaps to more ancient practices?

All these questions would remain unanswered. Like a widow who discovers only after her husband's death that she was being cheated on, I would have to reconcile myself to living the rest of my life with this other Alex, this Ali, whom I had never known. For in looking over these tattered bits of yellowed papers, the letters, sometimes unidentifiable because they had only nicknames for signatures, the dim faces in poor, unfocused snapshots—one of which might have been that of the man who fathered Alex—everything had seemed to me familiar and meaningful, yet it made no sense. I pored over them again and again, read and reread them, studied the faces carefully, making sure I had forgotten none in my search for the missing key that would elucidate once and for all the illogical machinations of fate. But nothing happened; the words remained just words, the pictures pictures, revealing little about this horrible mischance of human affairs.

Even today I wonder that I had the courage to disinter these parchments from the old chest Alex had left me, and to read them all to the end, going through every ghastly syllable.

I locked away the documents and sat out the night in dejection. Before dawn, I got up and began searching feverishly for the key to Alex's flat, which I knew had not yet been rented out because his cousin, who had stepped forward to claim it as his heir, was locked in a court dispute with the landlord of the building. I crossed the Bulak bridge, driven by an obscure desire to visit his apartment one last time. I could not help asking myself why I was so obsessed by the question of Alex's real identity. He had been dead two years; why did I not let him rest in peace? I felt suddenly very lonely listening to the croaking of toads and the chirping of crickets in the narrow strip of grass running along the riverbank. From somewhere unseen a quavering, melancholy verse of the Koran spun itself over the dark waters. Why was it that these beautiful chants had always had funerary associations for me that made them chilling? As I walked alone beneath the straggly palms of this miserable city, thoughts wheeled in my brain, thoughts of Alex, a dispossessed orphan, a failure maybe, yet accomplished to me, thoughts of myself in my fancy trappings—no one poorer or more desolate now. Unlike Alex, I had achieved success. But what did it all mean? Harvard: if that were all! I told myself I ought to find faith in life itself—in books, music, flowers, travels—in another love perhaps. Why was it that, richly endowed as I was with a capacity for living, I did not find mere faith in life sufficient?

I cannot remember exactly how I reached Alex's flat. It seemed to loom all at once before me in the dark. On his landing the flowerpots lay shattered, his snapdragons had sprawled on the floor, like dying voluptuaries, with their crimson tongues shriveled.

As I stepped into the shuttered gloom of his apartment, I asked myself once again what answers I hoped to find among these inanimate objects: the rickety closet with fleas jumping out of its rotten woodwork, the modest dresser with the half-empty cologne bottles, the creams, the bald hairbrush, the tweezers, the cotton balls and alcohol that he used to rub on his face, the manicure set, for Alex took great pains with his long-fingered, slender hands—these miserable possessions which his cousin had scorned and had fortunately left behind. And then that bed! That pitiful bed with the soiled mattress which had witnessed our shabby but hopeful love, and the pretty ruffled gauze window curtain—his one luxury—fluttering overhead. How often had I not lain there perfectly still, listening to the flies buzzing behind that curtain, patiently watching its slow intake and recoil, holding my breath in order not to wake Alex up, waiting till I could nestle in his arms.

Ensconced among the pillows, on his bare mattress, I could feel and taste the dust of the night that had just expired mingling with the oversweet fragrance of jasmine and that of sun-impacted oranges, as well as the smell of *sugu'*, a beef sausage eaten for breakfast by Egyptians of modest means. That odor of rancid fat, drifting in from the neighboring flats, which used to make my stomach turn whenever I visited Alex, brought back the image of the poor dressmaker huddling at our doorstep in her black *milaya*. Had she deliberately planted her baby, in a basket, outside of Nikolaides's house in the hope of finding his wife in a charitable mood? Perhaps even with him in the know? Or was Nikolaides's claim that Alex was not his son true?

I myself had, from the moment I began to consider the few, tattered documents Alex had left me, irresistibly regarded him as the son of Nikolaides. I was loath to give up the conviction that Alex belonged to an ancient and exalted race. His Greekness was an inseparable part of his physical attraction for me: he had persuaded me not to look at him in his present reduced circumstances but to look back at his glorious antecedents. It occurred to me only now, in this room filled with the nauseating reek of *sugu'*, that if I clung to this myth it was because I needed it as much as he did. I could not bear to think that Alex was nothing more than the son of that wretched woman in her shabby clothes. Perhaps Alex had known this and, fearing that I would snub him, had chosen to keep his secret to himself, to reveal it to me only after his death in this strange and disconcerting fashion.

In the weeks that followed, I returned often to Alex's flat on Antiquity Street in the evening, as though I hoped that, at a whim of fate, the man in the long, red silk scarf would reappear, just as suddenly as he had disappeared, stepping into that dead spring twilight—the heat, the dust, the flies, the smell of *sugu'*, of oranges, of jasmine. I found it hard to believe that the first time I had crossed over to his neighborhood there had hardly been anything that did not seem ugly to me, from the foul concrete cubicles—those incubators of human misery—to the shabby, narrow streets with their ragged figures; even the river, stagnant, slimy in this part of town, appeared to be a conducting medium of stench. The sordid uniform squalor of it all had seemed more than I could bear.

How strange that in looking back at it all, I was borne down by sadness, by regret for a lost world, a lost magic, a lost haven. My own house seemed so cold to me now! How deadeningly slowly the time passed there, with nothing to fill the silence at mealtimes but the sound of water being poured out of the carafe and the clatter of the dishes brought in on the monogrammed silver tray. The weight of those dishes, of my own suffering and bad conscience, the stiffness of those dead-white napkins set out in cones before the crystal glasses, the aching loneliness of that high-gloss, high-ceilinged dining room were more than I could endure.

I knew then that I must leave my father's house, never to return. I could not bear the sight of the somber English furniture in his study or the stern dignity of his official picture, in a red fez, which sat on his mahogany desk. I had often ridiculed that "flowerpot" on his head when I was a teenager, but lately, since his death, it had acquired a faint power to move me with a sense of time past, of glory departed—his and Egypt's—even though I knew that this glory had existed nowhere outside of its gilt frame.

God! I missed Father! I would have liked to take his wasted body tenderly in my arms, as I used to do every morning, and to place a soft kiss upon his ravaged cheek, feeling his hand, which was always cold, squeezing my arm affectionately in return. I missed not only the many things I had loved in him, but also what had most irritated me: the way he had dragged me, when I was already a grown woman, to his barber on rue Huysmans, in Paris, insisting that he cut my hair, wagging his finger remonstratively at me from behind the shop window as he left. What I would not have given to have him here, still alive, with all of his masculine whims, his patriarchal demands, his lack of consideration for everyone outside of himself. Was it possible that I had come to look at him as some kind of vulture, hovering over us, perched on that high-backed chair of his, looking down his imperious Turkish nose at everything and everyone—that long, slightly curved nose, which he was in the habit of tweaking when he thought something over, much to Mother's annoyance, and which had become exposed to its very roots by the gradual sinking of the flesh over the cheekbones, so that even when he sat in silence, there was something forbidding about the way the air whistled harshly through those prominent carved nostrils.

After Father had left us, I had wallowed in the misery of self-flagellation, recalling to mind that last day before my departure for the States, when I had planned a tea for him with a soufflé Rothschild, his favorite, which I would bake myself, as he was something of an epicure. I wanted to give him a tape of Leila Mourad's songs as a parting present, for of late he spoke incessantly of that Jewish-Egyptian singer and movie star, whom he had idolized as a boy—more recent events having begun to dim in his memory. I had exhausted myself searching for it, combing the streets and alleys, under a furious

Cairo sun, for her songs were long out of fashion. And when I finally offered it to him, instead of the grateful peck on the cheek I had expected, he let out a fierce growl, saying he had not asked me for it, I had no business getting it. Perhaps he had wanted to preserve intact in his memory—or imagination—the beautiful image of her he had cultivated for more than seventy years, which could not be held up to reality.

Now that he was gone, I listened every night in bed to her sweet, fluttering, insubstantial voice until an immense weariness began to steal over me and I fell asleep at last.

How I suffered at the thought that I had felt Father should go, that it was the only decent thing left for him to do. Indeed, such desolation, such a desperate sense of abandonment as I had never known—unless it was when Alex died.

For a long time, I was resolved not to visit Alex's grave: I told myself it was sentimental. In truth, I was terrified of cemeteries. But I felt a strange desire to go to Alexandria before leaving Egypt to bid farewell to his final resting place.

The summer season had not begun, Cairo had yet to

disgorge its huge crowds of pleasure seekers, whose furious gaiety gave Alexandria the air of a tawdry carnival. When I arrived, the city appeared to be hibernating: its illustrious sons had sunk into their dilapidated ancient mansions in silence: in the Rollo Villa, which had bustled, when I was a child, with the comings and goings of prosperous and prolific Jewish patricians, the only sign of life was a mangy black cat that crossed the west portico unhurriedly in the languid air. The seafront cafés had retreated indoors, and under a sky full of malific stars, the lonely shore rang with the shrill cries of gulls.

The Cairo bus had dropped me off at the station in front of the vestibule of the old Cecil, where a ventripotent former pasha, whom I recognized, sat amid the dead, dusty palms stuffing huge pieces of an *éclair au chocolat* into his flabby trumpeter's cheeks. On the long drive from the Cecil to the cemetery, I found nothing worthy of my nostalgia: by the silvery light of evening the sea seemed to have turned to ashes, and the King's palace on Muntazah Beach appeared to have fallen in ruins. A man with a tambourine was promenading his tethered red-assed baboon down the Grande Corniche; a solitary couple sat at Café Délices eating a desultory dinner of cold sandwiches; a few ragged boys were picking up cigarette stubs from the sidewalk; a posse of old Greeks, in traditional black sea caps, trudged their slow turtle walk up to the Billiard Palace.

By the time I reached the cemetery, night was closing in on it. As I fumbled in the dark for the latch of the gate, my knuckles knocked against it; I heard a small metallic chime—Alex's ring, I thought. What had he meant by that last gesture? At the time I had interpreted it as a pledge, but surely that wretched ring was intended for more than some shabby fulfillment in marriage. In retrospect, it appeared to me that in the restoring of that ring to a living finger he had tried to turn time back, to halt its inexorable advance, to freeze it. Another memory visited me: when, before my departure, I had dropped off a supply of L'Oréal hair color for Alex, along with the big tip needed to persuade the nurse to undertake so undignified a task after I was gone, she had confided to me that Alex had wept his heart out the previous night. Now I suspected that he had cried because he alone knew that he was destined never to leave that hospital.

While I was groping uncertainly through the stillness of the graveyard, in search of Alex's burial site, an immense archangel, black as thunder, beat up from the floating shadows. I was surprised and delighted to find that Alex rested not under a humble tombstone marked by a cross but under an opulent slab of Italian marble surmounted by that magnificent angel. I was glad also that his father was no longer around to prevent him from being buried in the family sepulcher, as he undoubtedly would have done had he outlived him; glad, too, that Alex's grave lay not in the crowded back area but in the first row, among the spacious vaults of Egypt's rich and powerful Christian families, who had spared no expense to achieve an impressive vulgarity of decoration complete with madonnas, cherubs, scrolls, and floral wreaths studded with semiprecious stones. Up front for once, I thought to myself. He would like that.

I stood there contemplating the angel, that spurious affirmation of immortality. A little plaque on the side of the tombstone caught my eye. It was coated with sand. Curious, I went to work on it, as one might on a fresco one was trying to restore, scratching off the encrusted sand, rubbing it with my saliva, polishing it with my handkerchief. And slowly there began to emerge the image of a handsome man, with an easy, swaggering manner, sporting a top hat and leaning on an ivory-handled cane—an image which, though faded from the sun, was undoubtedly that of Alex's father.

Looking at this face, inscrutable and serene, I could

not help asking myself once more who Alex really was: had he nothing more substantial for background than that shadowy figure, of a foster parent who might or might not have been his father? He seemed born of no woman, sprung of no childhood. He had flitted through my life, illuminating it for a moment, and then, like a butterfly that has completed its brief, pointless course, vanished for good.

My eyes scanned the names of neighboring tombstones: Gianaclis, Soursok, Bertolucci, Bellahofsky, Papasian, Winterhof . . . the remnants of the dwindling communities from Greece, Syria, Italy, White Russia, Armenia, Austria.

As I meandered among the rows of graves, bearing the legendary names, of dead captains, architects, engineers, bankers, business tycoons, and industrialists, who were as surely the founders of modern Alexandria in the nineteenth century as Alexander the Great was of classical Alexandria in 332 B.C.—the way one might peruse the rows of a museum gallery—my feet took me not only backward into the historical past but forward into the living present. And there arose before me palpable figures of old friends and acquaintances walking to and fro among these tombstones, among the ruins of cosmopolitan Egypt.

Now the tears came, but they were not for Alex. They were for potbellied Mr. Bertolucci, who made smacking sounds with his lips as he sucked the spaghetti off his fork and whom Mother had forbidden me to imitate when I was a child; for tall, lean Mr. Papasian, with the thin reddish mustache that ran like a streak of fire over his upper lip, whose daughter let me cheat from her in arithmetic; for fat and jolly Madame Bellahofsky, who, at the end of term, invited the whole class to her estate in King Mariout and played rousing Russian ballads on her balalaika for the parents, while we children took a dip in her pool.

Oddly enough, it was in searching about in this graveyard—so flamboyant by comparison to the elegant austerity of the neighboring Jewish cemetery, with its simple tombstones, whose haunted names echoed all the melancholy of years of exile in Spain, Russia, and Eastern Europe—for some clues to Alex's origins that I stumbled on the true meaning of our relationship. Perhaps it was not him I loved at all but his past—Egypt's past and my own. Perhaps I could not bear to give up as irretrievably lost those precious first years of my life. For unlike other children of the revolution who had been taught in Nasser's schools to suppress their reminiscences, to forget their playmates, to erase the hateful foreign names of their streets, squares, and trolley stops from their memory and replace them with valiant Arab ones, I had had parents who nursed my memories, stirred them up, whenever their pain had begun to flag.

In a sense, Alex had been Egypt for me, my own private Egypt. He had restored that magical sphere to me, complete and intact: thanks to him, I had been able to recover the blurred childhood images which Nasser had somehow tarnished—stolen from me. Those kisses by the seaside, the wind blowing up a golden curl onto Alex's white temples, summed up for me the many meanings of the old world. It was this world I inhabited to the exclusion of everywhere else. No wonder I felt comfortable among these silent, invisible presences. Here I knew I belonged: outside the cemetery gate I was a stranger.